There was someone ou_____ had to wait for the n___ _____ of the lighthouse before he could be sure. Yes, someone was there, more than one person. On the skyline at the top of the cliff humped shapes that could only be people were huddled together. Five or six of them, perhaps. Fools! Didn't they know it wasn't safe out there, there were enough barbed wire and notices about to warn off the summer visitors, anybody belonging to the town had more sense . . . If anyone fell from the top — Dan's eye was forced down the cliff face, as if by acknowledging the danger he could protect those stupid idiots from it. And then, as the lighthouse beam crossed over the cliff again, his stomach lurched. Someone was there on the rock face, flattened against it, fingers and toes fighting for purchase, moving slowly down towards the water. It was a boy, a small boy.

Janet McNeill

Janet McNeill is the well-known author of many bestselling books for young people. These include the 'Specs' series, THE BATTLE OF ST GEORGE WITHOUT, GOODBYE DOVE SQUARE, TOM'S TOWER, MUCH TOO MUCH MAGIC and THE MAGIC LOLLIPOP. She now lives in Bristol.

WE THREE KINGS

Janet McNeill

HODDER AND STOUGHTON
LONDON SYDNEY AUCKLAND

First published in 1974 by
Faber and Faber Ltd.
This edition 1992.

Reproduced by arrangement
with Faber and Faber Ltd.

British Library C.I.P.

A Catalogue record for this
book is available from the
British Library

ISBN 0-340-57740-1

Printed and bound in Great Britain
for Hodder Christian Paperbacks,
a division of Hodder and
Stoughton Ltd, Mill Road, Dunton
Green, Sevenoaks, Kent TN13 2YA
(Editorial Office: 47 Bedford
Square, London WC1B 3DP) by
Clays Ltd, St. Ives plc.

WE THREE KINGS

 *Chapter One*

Dan was the first to spot the list. He had every chance of doing so since he was spread out on the floor of the corridor, flat and peaceable as a kipper, when Mr Bingham came out of the staff-room to fix the list on the notice-board. Mr Bingham saw Dan, and halted with his drawing-pin held in mid air.

"What's the matter with you, then?"

"Nose bleed, sir." And Mrs Hartley asking inconvenient questions round the history class. Dan had an obliging nose and he hadn't done his homework. He dabbed his face with his handkerchief, turning it to give Mr Bingham a convincing view of the evidence.

"You virile young animals," Mr Bingham said, "all that fine red blood going to waste." He anchored his notice in a central position where no one could miss it, crowding poor Mrs Hartley's "Lost and Found" list on to the edge of the board. Not that anyone would overlook Mr Bingham's list; his handwriting, with those clever fancy wiggles and the circle instead of a dot on top of the letter "i", reached out from the paper and

7

grabbed hold of you and said, "Hi there! This is worth looking at!" And you looked, and it was.

Mr Bingham stepped back from the board to make sure that his notice was straight. "To Whom it May Concern!" he said sideways in Dan's direction, with an air of importance, as if he'd posted up the winning numbers for the Pools, or Saturday's team for the big match. Dan lay where he was and lolled a little more limply, refusing to show even a faint flicker of interest. Mr Bingham hovered hopefully for a moment, then beat a retreat to the staff-room, whistling "Scotland the Brave" briskly, between his teeth.

When he had gone Dan shuffled himself over in the direction of the notice-board. It would be safer to stay horizontal, for at any moment now the bell would ring to mark the end of morning school and Mrs Hartley would trot out of the classroom. He approached close enough to read the names, or at least to recognize them from their shape. He was pleased to see that his own name—D. T. Agnew—(he had been christened Daniel Thomas) was there. It was at the top of the list, in front of R. S. Agnew, his cousin Roger. Life at school and out of it tended to be a competition between Roger and himself. Their Dads were brothers. "How did Roger do?" Mum always wanted to know when he brought her any news of his own performance at school. She'd hear it all from Aunt Florence but she liked Dan to tell her first. Maybe it was the easy way Roger did everything that prickled Dan. "Sir Roger" they called him. Dan didn't mind Sid's name appearing at the head of games lists. Sid's hands

8

and feet had a private understanding with any ball that was ever thrown, kicked, hit or bounced. But on test lists, exam lists, prize lists, it was important to Dan that his name came ahead of Roger's.

On this particular list Dan knew he was at the top only because the names were written in alphabetical order, but even so it seemed proper and pleasing that he was there.

Funny how your own name, written out and exhibited in public daylight for everyone to read, gave you a pleasant nudge of recognition when you saw it. All your life long you'd have that name. Dan liked the sound of his name and its appearance on paper. Every day on his way to school he passed the shop with his father's name above it. "Samuel Agnew, Joiner and Cabinet Maker. Bicycle Repairs Promptly Executed." Probably his father had enjoyed putting those words there years ago, but the rain and the sea air had bleached them: the whole place looked starved for a coat of paint. The way things at home were going it didn't seem likely that they'd get it. It must be a couple of months since the windows of the shop had been cleaned; the salty wind had whitened them over, as if frost had visited the seaside town in September.

That was the bell that marked the end of morning school. Mrs Hartley braked on her way down the corridor, to ask Dan how he was feeling. There was a fishy and suspicious look in her eye. Dan gave her a brave smile and said he was much better, and she registered the bloodstained handkerchief and became

9

maternal. "Be sure and take it slowly when you get up, Dan," she advised, "easy does it."

Any time now the rest of them would come stampeding out of the class, bound for the dining-room. Dan decided he would pretend he hadn't read the list, didn't know anything about it. Let them discover it for themselves and find if their names were on it. Let them get excited if they felt so inclined. Mr Bingham wanted to see the following pupils in his classroom at the end of school. So what?

Dan knew the answer to that one. He had been watching and waiting for this list all week but he hadn't said anything about it to anybody. It was important to him not to appear too keen. Most of them, when they realized that this was the cast list for the Fourth Form play, would get lift-off and go into orbit straight away. They'd be starry-eyed from the word go. Everything they did would become a performance. Each time they walked through a door they would make an entrance. They'd be looking out for their reflections in pictures and windows and glass doors, in the way most of the girls did all the time. They would speak in stylish BBC voices, and a little more loudly than usual, so that the back row would be sure to hear.

Dan might have been doing all these things himself if it hadn't been for what had happened at the Talent Spotting Competition run by the Concert Party on the pier during August. He didn't think anybody at school, except Annette, had been there to see what happened, the townspeople didn't mix much with the holiday crowds, but somebody might have heard about it.

Even now when he allowed himself to remember it it made his toes open and shut and his stomach sag.

"Come on now, sonny, you're next. What treat have you got for us?" the man with the red nose and the plastic smile had asked him. "Speak up, what did you say?"

Dan told him what he'd said.

"Well! Very nice, I'm sure! William Shakespeare, the Bard himself! Ladies and gentlemen, you are in for a spot of culture. Silence please for my young friend— what name did you say it was, sonny?"

"Agnew, Dan Agnew."

"Fire ahead, Dan boy. It's all yours!"

And there he had stood, Dan Agnew, in the inescapable brightness of summer sunlight, giving a performance, competing with the seagulls and the distant band from the Promenade, making an exhibition of himself for the benefit of all those gawping red-faced strangers, the visitors who came down in their cars and coaches and by the train during the summer and spent their money, and behaved as if Dan's home town belonged to them.

"This day is called the feast of Crispian."

He knew his words well, he had practised them in front of the mirror in his bedroom the evening before. He had spoken the lines out loud. He was able to do this because his mother had the hoover going full blast downstairs, he knew she wouldn't hear. Dad was mooching about at the bottom of the garden, and it didn't make any difference if he heard or not. The mirror threw the words back at Dan's reflection. They had sounded magnificent.

"We few, we happy few, we band of brothers——" and right through to the end of the speech. He delivered it with power. He knew what tremendous things the words were saying, he could see the faces of the men of war, the glint of the lances, the hands tightening on them, could feel the nervous nagging impatience of that morning before the battle.

> *"And gentlemen in England now abed*
> *Shall think themselves accursed they were not*
> *   here!"*

Words like these couldn't fail him. He was sure he would transfix his audience. Even these dull city people, their eyes would gleam, perhaps grow wet, they would catch their breath. "Who is he?" someone would whisper, and a talent scout from television would scurry back stage afterwards to find out who he was.

It didn't work out like that. His audience turned their ice-creams and lollipops so that their tongues could harvest what had been melting on the other side. They adjusted their candy floss. They breathed out their warm boredom at him. For a couple of tottering moments he thought someone might laugh. Dan knew from experience that there was just a hair's breadth between what was heroic and noble and what was funny, but they didn't laugh. The thin applause they gave him faded immediately when they saw that Annette was hovering at the side of the stage, poised to follow him. She was doing her tap dancing, of course.

It would have to be Annette. The audience was smiling a welcome at her before she had pranced halfway across the stage. Those must have been her mother's eyelashes she was wearing. Annette's mother ran the Beauty Salon on the Promenade, and did a roaring business during the holiday season. The hot expensive smell that came from the door of the Salon killed the sea air stone dead. Dan was surprised that Annette didn't seem to have passed on to her cronies at school any account of his shameful experience on the pier during the holidays. Annette, whispering under her toffee-coloured hair, passed on most things.

Here she was now, here they all were, bearing down on him along the corridor like a herd of buffaloes. Joe and a couple of his stout lads, when they saw Dan still prostrate, hurled themselves in the direction of his stomach, but he scrambled to his feet just in time, and felt a warm thread of blood run down his lip.

At the sight of this Annette squealed. "I'm like that with blood," she said.

"I thought you said you watched the big fight last night."

"I did!"

"Well, if you watched that——?"

Mr Bingham's list had been spotted.

"I say, have you seen this?"

"What?"

"This list—Mr Bingham's."

"What about it?"

"Oh—that!" He attended to his nose, which was more important than any list.

Roger had drifted to the front and was making sure the list included his name before he showed anything more than a casual interest in it. Then he took charge and told them whose name was there and whose wasn't. Roger liked telling people. Dan stared out of a convenient window. Let Roger get on with it. The rest of them were waiting, unashamedly agog. Dan breathed on the window pane and drew complicated diagrams on it with his finger.

"Annette, you're here—and Mandy and Joan and Hazel and Phyllis and——" he recited the names of the girls Annette giggled around with, they did each other's hair in the cloakroom during the break and told each other's fortunes. They grew rosy in the face when the new French master passed them on the stairs. The Sob Sisters, the boys called them.

"And Joe and Co."

"Us?" Plainly they were surprised.

"I said so, didn't I?"

Dan thought Mr Bingham had made a mistake putting those names on the list. Anything that Joe and his lads were mixed up with was apt to end in confusion. Joe and Co. thrived on confusion. Uproar was Joe's speciality.

"Fred—you're here too!"

Fred gaped like a startled owl. "Me?"

"Take a look for yourself." Roger's finger stabbed the paper. It wasn't often that Fred's name appeared on any list except the Lost Property. Fred tried, he tried hard, but he was never really switched on to anything that mattered.

Someone said, "What do you suppose it's all about, anyway?"

Dan let them work it out for themselves. The suggestion soon came out: "Could be the cast for the play."

"So it could!"

The girls squealed, the boys whistled or sucked in their breath. Dan noticed that Roger just smiled. So he had known all along what the list was. Maybe like Dan he'd been expecting it every morning since the start of the autumn term a couple of weeks ago. Maybe this time Roger had been playing the same game as he had.

"What do you suppose it'll be this year?"

Last year the play had been *Twelfth Night*, the year before that it was scenes from *A Midsummer Night's Dream*.

"Hi, Megan! Your name's here."

Megan frowned and said, "Ha ha, very funny!"

"Take a look, then."

Megan looked and the frown grew deeper. She wedged her straight dark hair more tightly behind her ears. She would be a winner as Lady Macbeth, Dan thought. No damned spot would have a chance once Megan started to work on it. But she'd need something to get her started.

"And Dan. Oh—and Sid," Roger announced. Sid smiled right to the back of his handsome teeth. Of course Roger had kept Sid's name to the last on purpose. He knew Sid would be hoping his name was there, and he had left it as long as possible before he told him. Roger was like that with Sid, though Sid never seemed to notice. Sid rarely noticed anything except the things that were pleasant. Perhaps he found this more convenient.

"I expect we're doing *Othello*, that's why he wants you," Roger said in a nasty kind of way. But Sid continued to smile, as if Roger were awarding him a star part instead of referring to the colour of his skin. Sid's father kept the Maharajah Restaurant down by the Summer Pavilion. "Indian Dishes and Curries a Speciality." Each evening he stood just inside the revolving door, rubbing his long hands and looking perpetually pleasant. The smells that oozed out on to the pavement made the smell of sausage and mash on the doorstep of home as insipid as rice pudding.

"That's the lot then," Roger concluded, "except for Pete, of course." Pete was the Headmaster's son, he would have to be in it, nobody grudged him that. Nobody grudged Pete anything, not with his father perched up on a platform all the time and his mother wearing those mad hats and sounding like a female foghorn. Pete was an inoffensive, faceless kind of boy, always there but never out in the front. Probably he would be Third Soldier, or a Trainbearer, or Another Old Man. Pete never had much chance to be himself, he would find it easy to be Another Old Man.

Mrs Hartley bounded fussily out of the dining-room to inquire whether nobody was hungry today and why there was this traffic jam round the notice-board. Reluctantly they remembered their stomachs and pressed on. Possibly even Laurence Olivier had to eat.

Probably he didn't often have Toad in a Hole and Mashed Turnips, but that was what they were having. Not that it mattered, for nobody really tasted the meal. If it had been Larks' Tongues or Dinosaur Stew they wouldn't have noticed. They chewed their way through what was offered, thinking about Mr Bingham's list and what news he would have for them at the end of afternoon school. The fascinating itch to shed themselves and be transformed into strangers attacked them. They smelt greasepaint, not Turnips. What surprising changes might happen when they were somebody else! The thought of publicly escaping from themselves was alarming and wonderful. Any minute now they would be discovered. Mr Bingham had put them on that list because he knew they deserved to be there.

Dan, chasing his last slippery shred of peach round in the scrapings of his custard, remembered that after last year's play Mr Bingham had announced that next year they would take a rest from Shakespeare. He reminded Fred of this, and Fred passed it on to Roger. Roger said so what? Dan said so nothing, just that whatever it was it wouldn't be Shakespeare.

"Fancied yourself as Hamlet, did you?" Roger inquired. "Bad luck, the world will have to wait a while."

He took the last dollop of custard in an absent-minded kind of way, because it was there, not because he wanted it. Roger did everything with a swagger, even helping himself to custard. Dan didn't grudge it to him. He was hoping Mr Bingham had chosen a drama of Outer Space, the Victory of the Superbeings over the Creature from the Beyond. Roger could be the Creature, a Creature with a sinister swagger. Guess who would be the Commander of the victorious Superbeings? But what could you do with a type like Fred in outer space? Annette wouldn't fit into it very neatly either, and as for Megan—where would Mr Bingham find a use for her? If it was Greek Tragedy— he'd switched the telly off last week after only half an hour of it—she could be Cassandra. But no one would want Annette in Greek Tragedy, not even in the Chorus. It wasn't that kind of a Chorus. All "Woe, woe! Alas! Alas!", no giddy eyelashes and a wiggle and a kick. Perhaps a police court drama would suit them all better, lots of significant tight-lipped questions and answers, with skeletons falling out of cupboards in all directions. The girls could do the crying. But could Megan cry? No one had ever seen her at it. Annette could turn it off and on like a tap.

"Bet you it's Robin Hood," Joe said, licking his spoon and polishing it on his sleeve so that he could study his reflection in it. Lincoln Green would suit him and there would be plenty of fighting. Or it could be pantomime. Joe tried to decide which of the girls he would model himself on when he was cast as an Ugly Sister.

By the time they rose from the table and spilled out into the playground to kick half an hour away before the bell for afternoon school the boys had stopped trying to guess. It was too difficult. Already they felt a little uneasy in each other's company, not knowing

18

who was a Baddie and who the Goodies were, who was the principal lead and who was only part of a crowd or Voices Off. From the Girls' Cloakroom their laughter came annoyingly clear. Annette and the Sob Sisters thought it was funny. Perhaps it was. Perhaps the play would be a funny one, everyone being mistaken for somebody else and all getting more and more tangled up in each other's mistakes. Shakespeare did that quite a lot, but Mr Bingham had said it wouldn't be Shakespeare. Brian Rix did it too.

They scarcely noticed the maths lesson that came next on the time-table. Every one of them was already an unknown quantity, none of them knew any of the answers. Mr Hibbert droned on, and they were grateful to him for droning, because it filled up the time and because they could get ahead with their own thoughts. At last, at long long last, the bell released them into French Class.

It might as well have been Hebrew. Roger's accent, when it was his turn to read aloud, nearly tripped him up, but the rest of them mumbled and swallowed their way through. Even for the young French master Annette and her friends during that slow three-quarters of an hour never once turned pink or giggled. They had travelled ten years forward in their imaginations and were giving their first television interviews in the star dressing-room. "Little did I think——" and all the marvellous thoughts that had never entered their girlish minds. "Of course I never dreamed——" and the dreams they had not dared to dream but which had all come true.

"Everyone here?" Mr Bingham inquired. He was seated at his desk, large, magnificent and omnipotent as Zeus. He scanned their faces and they kept them stolid and unresponsive on purpose. They knew he wasn't seeing the people they were, but the characters he had ordained that they should be. Each of them was about to be born. Let him get on with it, and they would decide whether they were willing.

"I expect you're wondering what it's going to be this year," Mr Bingham suggested, trying to rouse some sign of interest from somebody.

"Not Shakespeare, you said not Shakespeare," Fred volunteered, wanting to be sure.

He agreed that it wasn't Shakespeare. "Something a great deal older than Shakespeare," he told them.

Was it going to be that Greek stuff after all? All that talking about fighting, but none of it happening where you could see it, doleful messengers of woe arriving from all directions? What else was older than Shakespeare? They rummaged through their memories.

"No guesses?" Mr Bingham prodded, tempting them to show a vestige of curiosity. No one uttered. They had begun to hate him blackly. They had begun to hate all adults in authority who had power and dominion over them.

"Christmas," Mr Bingham smiled, "doesn't Christmas suggest anything? Surely that must ring a bell for some of you?"

"A Panto, is it?" Joe asked hopefully.

Mr Bingham lifted the sheaf of papers from the desk in front of him and let it go, slopping the pages straight when they had fallen. "No, not a Panto," he told them, "a Nativity Play."

They gaped at him and gulped. It wasn't true! A Nativity Play? Them? He didn't mean it. He was being rude or funny, but a Nativity Play wasn't the sort of thing you were rude or funny about. Surely he must know! Hadn't he any sense? A Nativity Play at their age? They'd done all that stuff in the Junior School, they'd been shepherds and wise men and angels, padding around earnestly and being holy and enjoying it, because they were still young enough to enjoy being holy. Their Mums and Dads and Aunties and Grandmas had come to watch them taking part, and some of them had been seen wiping their eyes. Many of their family albums contained photographs of themselves wearing their cardboard crowns crooked, or carrying shepherds' crooks importantly, as if they had been rolled umbrellas. These photographs were now something to laugh over, politely, before they flicked the pages over to something else.

"Well, how does the idea appeal to you? Pretty challenging, eh?" Mr Bingham inquired, as if he'd expected they'd be all struck dumb with delight and enthusiasm.

"I don't suppose we'll be any good," Roger growled, and they were all grateful to him for finding something to say and for saying it.

Possibly by this time Mr Bingham had begun to get the message. He could hardly have missed it; like mules they looked. Plainly he hadn't expected hostility. He tightened his nose the way he did whenever things in class weren't going his way and said, "By the time I have finished with you, ladies and gentlemen, I promise that you will be superb." They recognised that this was a threat rather than a promise.

"Now I'll tell you who's who, and listen—repeat listen," he continued, and referred to his notes. He reeled the names off. "Mary—Megan; Joseph—Fred; the Angel Gabriel—Pete; Chief Shepherd—Joe; Chief Angel—Annette; the Three Kings: Caspar—Roger; Melchior—Dan; Baltazar—Sid. Everyone else, except regular members of choir and recorder players: boys— shepherds, girls—angels. First rehearsal Tuesday after school, second rehearsal Friday, and nobody—repeat nobody—is excused."

"But sir——"

"I said nobody. And let your parents know about it when you get home. We shall need all the help we can get with clothes and stage props. That will be Miss Hunt, of course, in the Art Room. Any parents with special skill will be particularly welcome. We will enlist your mother, Annette, for the make-up, and your father would give us a hand, wouldn't he, Dan, with the shepherds' crooks. I know he'd make a good job of those."

Dan made a noise in his throat and felt his face flame. It was a pity that at that moment he happened to look across at Roger. Roger was grinning, sticking an elbow into the ribs of the boy standing beside him, and jerking his head in Dan's direction. "That's a bit of a laugh, that is," the grin meant. Dan's face could not reach a deeper shade of red but he felt the insides of his hands grow sticky. One of these days he'd belt Roger. But even when they were kids playing on the floor together it was Roger who did the belting. This time Dan would perhaps have belted him, but Roger happened to be right. Roger's Mum was Aunt Florence, married to Dad's brother Bill, and she knew better than most how things were at home. It was odd how those two could be friends, his own everyday Mum and pretty dressy Aunt Florence, who smelt of perfume and cigarettes when she kissed you, which she always did.

Mr Bingham was harvesting his personal belongings from the desk and stowing them in his brief-case. He didn't speak as he left the room. They didn't speak. They listened to his footsteps all the way along the corridor, and no one budged until they had heard the door of the staff-room slam.

At last Fred croaked, " 'Jesus wants me for a Sunbeam!' " and Annette told him that was rude, and Fred said it wasn't, it was a hymn in case she didn't know, and Pete chipped in that it was a good job somebody wanted him for something, and then their tongues unfroze and everybody began to talk at once.

Chapter Two

Their indignation wasn't as noisy or as rich as it might have been because they felt uncomfortable as well as angry. What had happened was unfair. Church, or anything to do with Church, was always like that. You couldn't let off steam and shout or throw things no matter how riotous and rebellious you were feeling. Few of them were in Church often, except Christmas and maybe Easter, but you couldn't be funny about Church the way you could be funny about most things. If you tried to be, grown-ups soon told you off, even if they didn't go much themselves. Anyway, Church wasn't funny. It was one of the things you had to be solemn about, like blind people or an animal left to starve, or like dying. And the habit of reverence persisted.

"A Nativity Play mightn't be so bad after all," Fred ventured, taking a chance that someone would share his enthusiasm.

"It'll be terrible!"

"Why? I don't know what you're on about!"

"All holy and solemn! I daresay it'll suit you all right but not us!"

"Of course it'll suit Fred! All cosy and blessed, like it is at the Mission every summer when he goes and gets saved! Three summers running Fred's been saved! That's why Mr Bingham picked him for Joseph!"

Fred grinned; he was aching for someone to tell him how important Joseph was.

"Joseph only has to stand at the back," Megan said sourly, and he made a face at her and dried up.

"Mr Bingham's pulling a fast one on us, do you think?" Joe growled. No chance of Sherwood Forest now, no chance of raising a giggle as an Ugly Sister.

"What do you mean? A fast one?"

"Like Mr Everard—remember?"

Indeed they remembered. Mr Everard had come one spring term to help with junior games and gymnastics. They liked him from the start, he made them laugh, they marvelled at his muscles. He invited some of them round to his digs one evening. "Sandwiches and a sing-song," he said. He had rooms in Mrs Hutchin's house above the Post Office. They went in a body and found they had walked straight into an ambush. In between the jokes and the sandwiches Mr Everard was being earnest, now he was being holy. The music on the piano proved to be an album of Gospel Choruses. Their toes curled, they tried not to look at each other, and filled their mouths with sandwiches to make themselves dumb. Mr Everard flipped the pages of the music over, trying to find a Chorus they knew. They chewed and shook their heads, looked challengingly at Fred. This was his province. At last Fred piped an unwilling treble to Mr Everard's fruity baritone.

Now Mr Everard had done enough singing, he got up to seize another sandwich, bite into it, and was suddenly kneeling on Mrs Hutchin's carpet, inviting them to join him. They hadn't seen this coming, he had gone down on his knees in one fluid athletic movement. Stiff-kneed and stiff-necked they stayed erect, still unable to look at each other or to take their eyes off Mr Everard. This sort of behaviour was an offence. You didn't pray with your mouth full, you didn't flop down in a drawing-room without any warning. Praying ought to be done in Church, at a distance, by someone else, using beautiful words that were hard to understand. This was too near, too sudden, much too familiar. Mr Everard was trespassing on something that needed to be protected, but they didn't know what it was or how to tell him. Six inches of hairy leg were showing above Mr Everard's socks. The carpet on which he knelt was sprinkled with crumbs. His voice went on and on, punctuated by the chirp of Mrs Hutchin's budgie.

Roger had caught Dan's eye.

"We've got to get out of here!" he mouthed.

"Now's our chance!"

It was no more ill-mannered of them to take their chance than it was of Mr Everard to give it to them. Roger and Dan shepherded the rest of them through the door. They were halfway down the stairs when they heard a vigorous "Amen!" They ran the rest of the way. Nobody talked about it afterwards. Mr Everard only stayed for a couple of terms.

"Anyway, why Megan for Mary?" one of the girls

was asking, and they turned from past embarrassments to the present.

"I'll be terrible!" Megan growled and nobody disagreed with her.

"It ought to have been Annette!"

Annette grew pink and fluffed her hair out, looking pleased.

"Anybody would be better than Megan—even Margie. My Mum had a Christmas card last Christmas where Mary was the image of fat Margie."

Margie hesitated, uncertain whether to look complimented or insulted, and succeeding only in looking fat.

"I'll tell you why Mr Bingham picked on Megan—he's seen her pushing the pram, that's why!"

"I have to push the pram, my Mum makes me!" Megan snarled.

Since her big sister Sylvie had brought the baby home Megan was landed with the pram most evenings. You saw her scudding full pelt along the sea front with it, as if people wouldn't notice her as much if she went past in a hurry, or doing laps round the Park when there weren't many other prams about. Her big sister Sylvie sang with a Group in the city; they were just beginning to make a name for themselves. It looked as if the baby might be a fixture.

"Just the job for us, the Three Kings, I don't think," Roger grumbled at Dan. Sid heard this and said he was the Third King and please to remember and thank you, and Roger told him he had to be the Third King, hadn't he, meaning there was no one else whose skin was the right colour.

"Clout him, why don't you?" Joe prodded, but Sid just widened his smile and said what good did clouting do, and all Kings were equal. Sid was like that.

" 'While humble shepherds washed their socks', that's me," Joe mocked, and someone suggested that sheep would be a change from donkeys, anyway. Big Joe, Joe's father, owned the donkeys which gave rides on the beach during the summer and Joe helped him. Sheep would be easy after donkeys.

The Sob Sisters were already discussing what they would do about wings. "Angels' wings are feathery, not gauzey like fairies."

"Grow them, why don't you?" Joe said, and ducked just in time.

Fred debated whether Joseph would qualify for a halo.

"The Angel Gabriel has a halo, that's for sure. You could borrow one of your Mum's hats, Pete!"

"Oh, stuff it!" Peter shuddered, wishing he had been chosen for Another Old Man or Voices Off.

In twos and threes, doubtful, pleased or indignant, still chewing over Mr Bingham's surprising choice, the possibility of rigging up a star, the impossibility of camels, they collected their bicycles from the shed or scuffed their way on foot out on to the road.

Roger was waiting for Dan, part of their way home lay together. "Odd kind of a circus," Roger commented. "I suppose one of us is First King."

"If it's a procession someone has to walk in front," Dan conceded.

"The black chap comes at the back, anyway."

"It doesn't matter who's in front." But it mattered just as much as it used to matter when they were kids in each other's nurseries, deciding who would be Cowboys and who would be Indians and whose turn it was to win.

A gaggle of juniors were hanging around the school gate. Unexpectedly Roger joined them. "Be seeing you." This suited Dan. He was glad to be on his own. Kings ought to come one at a time.

The school was built on a hillside a little distance from the town. The road down to the sea-front passed the field where Big Joe kept his donkeys when the season was over. The big barn in the field gave the animals cover during the worst of the winter. They were social beasts and missed the stir and bustle of the beach. Now they pushed their rough necks across the gate, snuffling goodwill. Dan rubbed their noses.

Now his route took him along the sea-front. This afternoon it was almost deserted. This was the way he liked it. The sea sounded wild and sad, not the tame water in which holiday makers swam and squealed and children trailed their boats. The tide was coming up the sand fast, green glass turned to lace as each wave tipped over.

A couple of months ago this sand would have been packed tight with deck chairs, sprinkled all over with picnic parties, studded with castles and scarred with moats and the tracks of the donkeys, strewn with paper bags, orange peel, lollipop sticks. Now, except for the zigzag of seagulls' feet the beach was as unmarked as it had been when this morning's outgoing tide had uncovered it. The brown festoons of seaweed lay where the water had dropped them.

Because the sky was overcast the daylight had already begun to fade, and in a few of the houses the lights were lit. At this time of year these were the honest lights of home, not the crazy confusion of red and green and blue that winked and spun on summer evenings, spelling out the ways in which the visitors could spend their money. The awnings in front of the shops had been taken down and stored, the racks of postcards and toys no longer stood on the pavement, inviting customers. The boating lake was deserted except for the plastic gnomes and storks, the amusement arcade was silent, no chance for the last coin in your pocket to make a millionaire of you. Two of the chip shops were shuttered, and no table-cloths gleamed through the boarding-house windows. The exhausted landladies had waved good-bye to the last of their guests and had taken themselves off on their own holidays.

Dan liked this feeling of emptiness. He could smell the sea, unmixed with any whiff of hot dogs or chips. A solitary gull idled a few feet above his head, crying mournfully, and he loved it. Already some of the lights were lit in the big Hotel at the further end of the bay. A couple of dozen wealthy people stayed there throughout the winter, when the bus tours had dried up. It was because of her work at the Hotel that the hoover had been busy at home the evening Dan was practising his Shakespeare. Mum was catching up. She was always catching up, as if she proved something to herself by being twice as busy since Dan's father had come to a full stop.

A car drew in smoothly at Dan's elbow, cleverly matching its pace with his own. Uncle Bill on his way home from his office in the city. The building trade was booming. The car was this year's model. Uncle Bill had built himself a fine house at the far end of the town. "The air out there's lovely," Aunt Florence was fond of telling Mum.

"Hiya!"

Dan said, "Oh. Hallo."

"Hop in!" Uncle Bill commanded, large and smiling like he always was. "I'll take you as far as your corner."

Dan obeyed, determined not to be impressed, not to sink too deeply into these impossibly soft seats.

"Late this evening, aren't you?"

"There was a meeting after school."

"They work you hard at that place," Uncle Bill suggested, "but I daresay you keep up all right. Hard work never hurt anyone, you don't get far in this world without it, that's what I tell Roger. He's on the road, is he?"

"I think he stayed to talk to someone." Let Roger explain for himself what business he had with those kids.

"Always plenty to say for himself, our Roger," Uncle Bill agreed. He stopped the car at the corner to allow Dan to get out. "And tell your father to drop in any time he's around. Always a welcome on the mat, tell him that!"

Dan slammed the door of the car a little more vigorously than Uncle Bill would have liked, and turned towards home.

This was the corner where the steepest road from the upland countryside joined the sea-front. Dan wondered if he would ever go past it now without remembering. It was a bad corner. It had been known to be a bad corner, accidents had happened there before the June evening three months ago when Megan's young brother Philip had come careering down the hill, whooping and swooping, on his bicycle. The long hill was a favourite challenge for boys and their bicycles, they knew every twist and trick of the descent, they knew how long it was possible to come at full speed, and which was the last moment when brakes must be eased in, and the flying hedges pulled to an easy pace.

Philip Lloyd had let that last moment go by. He had crashed at full speed into the sea wall and was unconscious when the ambulance reached him. It would be a long job, they said at the hospital, it was possible he might learn to walk again. The machine was so battered that it had been impossible to establish the state of the brakes. The local newspaper suggested that the sun might have been in the boy's eyes, and added a recommendation that youngsters' bicycles should be overhauled at regular intervals.

Dan knew that at the time of the accident the evening sun at this corner couldn't have dazzled a cyclist's eyes. He also knew that Philip's bicycle had been in his father's shop for an overhaul at the beginning of the week. Everyone in the town knew this too.

As he went past the telephone booths Dan found he was treading on broken glass. So the Wreckers had been at it again. The Wreckers, that was the name the town had given to the gang, whoever they were, who had been active all year. Street signs were broken, awnings slashed, window boxes uprooted, you name it, they wrecked it. The local police hadn't a chance against these wily workers of destruction. This time it had been the turn of the telephone booths.

Now Dan had reached his father's shop. He went past it quickly, telling himself that he knew there wouldn't be any light in the window or any sight or sound of activity, so that he could dodge the sick feeling he got in his stomach if he forgot to be prepared for disappointment. He used to enjoy dropping into the shop on his way home from school, smelling the sharp smell of newly-cut timber, of paint or enamel, as he opened the door and stood without speaking until his father looked up from whatever work absorbed him and saw that Dan was there.

Of course there was no light in the workshop tonight. He was nearly home now. Home was the end house of the tall old-fashioned terrace of houses beside the railway bridge, just before the railway entered the station. One wall of the house was built right against the bridge. Dan's bedroom was on this side. Whenever a train crossed the bridge his room shivered, as if the train picked up the little house in its teeth and shook it gently before it set it down again. Dan liked to be awake in the early morning when the newspaper-and-milk train arrived. The square of light reflected from his bedroom

33

mirror trembled against the wallpaper and sometimes the window pane rattled.

"Late tonight, aren't you? And mind the floor, I've just done it over." Mum was knitting and working at the crossword while she waited for the washing machine to complete its final spin.

"Hallo, Dad."

"Hallo." Dad didn't turn away from the television. His hands were white now, even the thumbs.

"I was just saying to your father he ought to take a turn along the road to meet you, a breath of fresh air always does you good, doesn't it, Dad?"

"That's right."

Mum said, "You don't really want this rubbish on, do you, Dad?" and got up to turn the television off. "Mind what you're doing with that cigarette ash," she told him.

"Well, what kept you late?" she wanted to know, and Dan told her about Mr Bingham's list and the Nativity Play.

"A Nativity Play?"

"Joe was hoping it would be Robin Hood or a Pantomime."

His father hadn't looked at him or smiled. He must make what he was saying matter to Dad.

"Remember the time we went to the Panto, Dad? A couple of years ago?"

"Of course he remembers, don't you, Dad?" Mum supplied.

"It was just Dad and me. You were out with Aunt Florence. You remember the clowns, Dad? The big one who put the little one into the waste paper basket? You must remember!" They had laughed themselves sore over that clown, all the way home they had laughed.

"Your Dad told me about it afterwards. Of course he remembers," Mum repeated. "This Nativity Play—you're in it, are you?"

"Yes."

"Did you hear that, Dad? Dan's in the school play. What part are you doing?"

"I'm to be one of the Three Kings."

"Well now! Which one? First King, are you?"

Here we go again. "I don't know about First. I'm King Melchior, Mr Bingham said."

His mother sniffed. "Oh—Melchior—he's the old one." Mum knew a lot about things like that, between her crosswords and having been at Sunday School when she was little.

"I didn't know Melchior was old."

"Who's to be Caspar?"

"That's Roger. What's Caspar like?"

"He's the one who leads and brings gold." He would be, Dan thought sourly.

"And Sid is Baltazar."

"Well, he would have to be, wouldn't he? And it saves some other lad having to get his face blacked."

"Sid's all right, Mum."

"I didn't say he wasn't, did I? Did you hear that, Dad? Roger and Dan are to be Kings. Roger is the First King, the one who leads and brings gold."

"Why Roger?" Dad asked.

"It's Mr Bingham who chooses."

His mother asked about the other parts and he told her. "Megan?" she puzzled when he said who had been chosen for Mary.

"Everyone thought it should have been Annette."

"Did you hear that, Dad? Dan says Megan Lloyd's chosen to be Mary."

Of course Dad had heard. Megan Lloyd, Philip's sister, Mum didn't have to spell it out like that. The Lloyd family was the last thing Dad would want to talk about. Not that anything seemed to mean very much to him now. If he heard what she said he agreed with it. If he didn't hear, his silence made no difference to her.

Dan ached for things to be the way they used to be at home, easy and ordinary, not this terrible, careful politeness. Big Joe, who lived with his wife and family in a caravan in the field full of donkeys, argued with Mrs Joe. He shouted at her. She shouted at him. You heard them hard at it when you were going past. In the evening you saw them going out to The Holly Tree, Mrs Joe all dolled up and both as happy as Larry.

There must be some way of making Dad take notice of something. You couldn't let what had happened wipe out the whole history and language and pattern of a family. Maybe the sun had after all jumped across the sky and dazzled Philip Lloyd's eyes. Of course Dad remembered those clowns.

"Everyone is to be asked to help, Dad, Mr Bingham said so. People who aren't in the play will be in the choir or playing their recorders. Miss Hunt and the Art Department are doing the costumes and the scenery. Anyone in the town who can help will be helping." He drew a deep breath. "I told Mr Bingham you would make the crooks for the shepherds."

Neither Dad nor Mum spoke. For once Mum was waiting for Dad to speak first. Go on—say something.

"Mr Bingham said he knew you would make a good job of them, Dad," Dan added.

There was no noise in the room except the dry rasp of his father's hands.

"Well of course he'll make a good job of it, won't you, Dad?" Mum said at last. "Anything your father does he makes a good job of it."

Dan knew there was one more thing he could say and he said it. "When Mr Bingham said Dad would make a good job of the crooks for the shepherds Roger seemed to think it was funny."

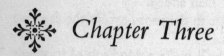 *Chapter Three*

"Hold it a minute, Roger, hold it," Mr Bingham directed, massaging the bony part of his nose briskly between his finger and thumb. "Now tell me, just what do you imagine you are doing?"

Roger bristled and his lower lip thickened. At the first rehearsal they had simply sat at their desks and read the play through. This had been dull but easy. Now, script in hand, they were plotting the movements. "I am approaching with awe, bearing gifts," Roger said, "at least that's what it says here that I'm supposed to do."

" 'Approaching with awe?' From where I am it looks much more as if you were an astronaut out on a moon walk," Mr Bingham told him, and a dry giggle ran through the rest of the actors, even though they were on Roger's side. Mr Bingham was right, Roger did look like that, gliding across the classroom with his knees bent a little and his head poked forward, lifting and lowering each foot as if he were riding an invisible bicycle. His two pages trotted alongside. Each of the Kings had been furnished with a couple of juniors to act as pages.

"Anyway, what about these gifts you're meant to be bearing?" Mr Bingham wanted to know.

"I can't bear gifts when I've got to keep holding my script."

"I was under the impression that you had two hands."

Roger's face became a sulky beetroot colour. He didn't like being mocked in public. "I haven't got a gift to bring."

"Use your imagination. Anything will do—anything." Mr Bingham looked about him. "Here, take this!" He seized a dictionary from his desk and thrust it at Roger, then turned to Dan and Sid who were lined up close behind. "You two—get something in your hands, can't you?"

Dan grabbed somebody's lunch box, which was nearest. Sid furnished himself with the board rubber.

"Myrrh, careful with it, it's pricey stuff," Mr Bingham warned, smiling to make sure Sid knew it was a joke. Masters were like that with Sid, as if they wanted to assure him they didn't mind his being the colour he was. "Now, four steps before you turn, pages a little behind, everyone bow your heads as you approach."

"Wouldn't our gifts be carried by the pages, that's what they're there for, isn't it?" Roger asked, feeling a fool with his golden dictionary.

"Your pages are there to attend your persons and to look after the camels. You carry your own gifts."

Roger objected, "Even when we're Kings?"

"Kings come to do homage. And don't forget what I told you about bowing your head."

Roger remarked that if he bowed his head his crown

would be likely to fall off, but Mr Bingham assured him firmly that nothing—repeat, nothing—would fall off after Miss Hunt and her team had finished with it.

"Come on now, get moving."

They approached with awe a second time. One of Dan's pages had begun to hiccup nervously. Dan, bracing himself for the next hiccup, got out of step.

"More like the slow movement in a Zulu war dance, that was," Mr. Bingham remarked. "Sid's the only one of you who looks as if he might have a drop of royal blood in his veins. And can't you put a stopper in those hiccups?"

Things were not going well. The mild excitement which had infected them had dissolved and been followed by a cold heavy gloom. It wasn't anybody's fault. Nobody had been wildly enthusiastic when the rehearsal started, but at least they were ready to do a reasonable proportion of what was asked of them. The play-reading in class the previous week had been flat but they had told themselves it would be different when they began to move about. Things would start happening.

Moving didn't make any difference, no one was transformed. To be required to say words and move at the same time became impossibly complicated. Their tongues thickened, their knees grew stiff, even putting one foot in front of the other was an artificial kind of manoeuvre. Words printed clearly enough on paper turned out hopelessly tangled when they were spoken, or stilted like the mottoes out of crackers. The skin of their faces tingled as if it had been scrubbed, and they avoided looking at each other.

Pete's performance as the Angel Gabriel had been the big surprise. He had modelled himself on his father, his official platform manner, and delivered his words with all the Headmaster's weight and authority. Megan, as Mary, had plainly been terrified. There she was now in the stable, brooding and uneasy, holding a rolled-up blazer in her arms as if it had been a bundle of washing, and with that worry line running down between her eyes. Joseph, presiding from the back, looked thoroughly relaxed and at ease. Fred was happy.

The angels had got their big scene over early and were now grouped in the background. Each of them had washed her hair the evening before and had spent every spare moment brushing it. It flowed below their shoulders in every shade of yellow and gold, silver-gold, copper, toffee colour, nut brown, mouse, leaf brown, black, tawny, chestnut and honest carrot. It cascaded and swung like silk, like candy floss, like sheaves of corn, like smooth polished rivers. And they knew their words, too. Obviously they had rehearsed their glad tidings of great joy in private beforehand. They delivered them unanimously, without faltering, but the words sounded more like an advertisement on commercial television for some wonder product than a pronouncement from heaven.

The shepherds' reception of the angels hadn't satisfied Mr Bingham. "What would you feel like," he asked Joe, "if some night when you were rounding up your father's donkeys in the field a whacking great angel

41

appeared out of the sky?" Joe gave a wolf whistle, but Mr Bingham said that wasn't what he wanted either. " 'They were sore afraid,' " he said, "remember that," and Joe and the other shepherds nudged each other and their mouths fell open.

"You look more like sheep than shepherds," Mr Bingham told them testily, "and couldn't you, Joe, sound more like a countryman?" Joe, who had the speaking part, put on a touch of the Archers, and everyone laughed and they had to try it again.

And now it was the turn of the Kings, and no sign yet that things were improving. Roger was still attempting to stalk like royalty, Dan's page had stopped hiccuping but had begun to sniff.

"Not so lively—remember you are an exceedingly old gentleman, Melchior," Mr Bingham reminded him.

"Yes, I know," Dan said miserably, trying to feel elderly and regal and humble all at the same time and only succeeding in feeling confused and foolish. His left foot was starting pins and needles. The lunch box that he was holding smelt of cheese. This reminded him that he was hungry. Hamlet would have been a great deal easier than this. Hamlet only had to feel one thing at a time.

None of the cast was happy. They all had the uncomfortable feeling that a Nativity Play, if they were going to be any good at it, should have made them feel solemn right away, the way going into Church made them feel solemn, but this wasn't working. Here they were, willing to be changed into the characters in a stained-glass window, which would have been pleasant and convenient, but nobody had really changed from what he or she was every day in the week. There was none of the expected camouflage of holiness or history to help them. Perhaps it would be better when the recorder players and the carol singers, who were re-hearsing with the music master, had joined them.

Mr Bingham wasn't helping much either. At the start of the rehearsal some of his comments had been funny, and a few people had laughed, but no one felt like laughing now. Dan, following closely on Roger (three steps, pause, three more steps, turn, pause, kneel down) thought that the hind legs of a pantomime horse would have given him more of a chance to act than this did, and that it was a pity it had to be Roger who was in front. If Mr Bingham had jollied them along things mightn't have turned out so bad, a dramatic spark could have been struck somewhere, but he seemed to have become hostile, as if already his confidence in the choice of play was cooling, and he was taking it out on them. Mr Bingham was accus-tomed to pull things off in style. There wasn't a glimmer of style here. He knew he'd backed a non-starter.

"Break it up," he told them wearily, "and everyone learns their words before next rehearsal—and when I say everyone that's what I mean."

They were glad to be given their release. The angels took out their pocket combs and made off in a body, chattering, to the cloakroom mirrors, to find out what they had really looked like before it wore off. Joe and his shepherds deserted their fields and flocks and started half a dozen cheerful private battles to ease their feelings.

Dan, as he left the classroom, passed Roger, who was holding one of his pages (it was little Ronnie Simpson) by the ear. It couldn't have been comfortable, the kid looked scared as a rabbit, his eyes were screwed up with the pain.

Dan overheard Roger saying, "Because I tell you to, that's why. And you know who I am, don't you? I am the King. Well—do you know or don't you? Go on—say it?"

"Because you say so, Roger. Because you are the King," Ronnie mumbled, stiffening himself for the next yank on his ear.

"And you know what happens to you if you don't?"

Dan would have stopped to find out what the trouble was and to make sure the kid got away, but he'd had about enough of Roger and his kingly habits for one day. And this was Friday. His mother worked late at the Hotel on Friday afternoons. She left a list of errands for him in the kitchen, he must get home to collect it and come back again to the shops before they closed.

The list and money were waiting on the table. Dad was in his chair. He hadn't even switched on the box. He didn't move or look up. The furniture looked more lively than he did.

"I'm back, Dad."

"Yes."

"Mum left the list, did she?"

"It's there. And the money."

44

Dan picked them up slowly, making a business of it. "Is there anything you want me to get for you, Dad?"

"No." His father's fingernail tapped out a rhythm on the arm of the chair, over and over, softly, again and again.

"The strap on my schoolbag has come loose again, Dad. It needs fixing," Dan said, and waited for the miracle. It would be a quite simple miracle, not a great deal to ask. All it needed was for Dad to say, "Give it over here," and stretch a long arm out for the schoolbag, and another arm to the box where he kept his awl and the waxed end.

"The strap, it needs fixing," Dan repeated.

"Not a hard job," his father said, without any change of voice or attitude. It wasn't a day for miracles. The broken strap would join the list of all the other things that had failed to become important. If Dad didn't stop tapping his finger-nail like that an explosion would blow the house to smithereens. Tap tap. Tap tap tap.

"We had a rehearsal for the play today."

"Oh yes."

"Terrible it was; we were terrible."

You told yourself it couldn't go on like this but it did. Probably there was some way of stopping it from hurting, if you could find it, but if it stopped hurting something else would be finished, too. Better to let it hurt. Tap tap. Tap tap tap.

"Roger was the worst of the lot. Lousy, he was. Mr Bingham fairly blew his top, he was so bad."

His father didn't answer but the tapping had stopped. Dan slid the list and the money into his pocket and turned out of the house and back in the direction of the shops.

Outside the grocery shop he spotted Megan who had just finished loading her heap of purchases into the pram. She spat out the piece of hair she was chewing and frowned "Hallo" sideways at him as he passed her, but he pretended he hadn't heard. He decided that he would spend a long time getting his own order, then she would be well out of the way before he came out. He took as long as he could, even counting his change before he left the shop and fingering through the box of fireworks that lay on the counter ready for Bonfire Night, until his hands smelt pleasantly of gunpowder. He hadn't done his budgeting yet, Dad had forgotten to slip him the extra pocket money to buy this year's supply of fireworks and he felt awkward about asking.

It was growing dark as he came out of the shop, but the lights shining from the window, past the tins of soup and gravy mix and the pyramid of oranges, showed him that Megan and the pram were still there. He decided to be blind or in a frantic hurry or else plain rude, it wouldn't matter much with Megan, maybe she wouldn't even notice. He was surprised when she called, "Hi, Dan!"

He slowed and said, "Hi yourself," as crossly as he could.

"Hang on a minute!"

"What's up?"

"The brake of this pram has jammed."

"Then unjam it."

"I can't, you nit!"

"You just have to give it a yank and a shove."

"I know, but I can't."

Reluctantly he set his shopping bag down on the pavement, propping it carefully against the wall; there were eggs in it. He crouched beside the pram, feeling for the brake mechanism. The baby was bouncing and whooping, which didn't help. The pram rocked and his grip slipped.

"Tell him to put a sock in it, would you? How can I get anything done with him carrying on like that?"

"You tell him yourself," Megan shrugged. She said, "Shut up, do you hear?" to the baby, but this only encouraged him to further enthusiasm.

"You aren't much use, are you?" Dan mocked. "Or he must be getting the wrong kind of vitamins. What's his name, anyway?"

"We just call him the Kid at home."

There were four girls of the Lloyd family still at home, and the two boys now that Philip was in hospital. People in the town said it must help Mrs Lloyd, after her trouble with Philip's accident, to have a baby in the house. Mrs Lloyd was a large vague woman, you never noticed her much because of the tribe of children who were always in noisy orbit round her.

The pram had stopped rocking. But now the Kid was sagging sideways and didn't seem able to right himself.

"Shouldn't you straighten him up or something?" Dan asked.

"If I do he'll only start rocking again."

"You'd better do something."

Bad-temperedly Megan pulled the Kid into a more satisfactory position.

"You're supposed to be handier with babies in the play," Dan told her.

"It'll be different with a doll. And you'd better get a move on and fix that brake quick, Dan, for pity's sake. Look who's coming!"

Dan looked and saw the sense of what she said. The old people from Eventide Home on the sea-front were drifting along the shops in twos and threes, as if a jumble sale was out on the loose. "The Oldies" the town called these people. Dan always avoided looking in at the windows of Eventide because if once you looked in and saw them all sitting around in their armchairs, like rows of plants, it was hard not to stare. You didn't believe that they were real. You weren't sure if you wanted to believe it. You were afraid you would laugh, and being old was another of the things you weren't supposed to laugh at. These ladies and gentlemen had no friends or families with whom they could live, so they lived at Eventide Home together until they died. They were always laughing among themselves, chirpy as sparrows, as if things were funny. You hardly ever saw them but they were laughing. They went to each other's funerals as if they'd been asked to a party.

They were laughing now, opening little packages and paper bags to show each other what they had bought, comparing purchases and exclaiming over them. Old Mr Anstruther was in the middle, the ladies hemmed him in. He was smaller than any of the ladies, just a wisp with a hat on. The ladies were accustomed to hem Mr Anstruther in when they were returning from a shopping expedition; the little man had been known to slip off into The Holly Tree and spend an hour or two in the Saloon Bar, returning to Eventide full of jokes and cheerful songs, and distressing dear Matron very much. The ladies felt it was their duty to protect him from temptation.

"There's Melchior for you," Megan said, pulling a face at Dan and jerking her thumb towards Mr Anstruther. Dan pretended he hadn't heard. He kept his head down, and tried to think of Moses in the stained-glass window in the Church, very old and very substantial, very noble and wise. That was Melchior, not an elderly little comic giggling into a paper bag. The brake of the pram wouldn't move. He wished that he had his father's hands, the brake would have presented no problem to them. As far back as he could remember Dan had never known anything broken or damaged that his father's hands couldn't put right.

"Oh Dan, hasn't it budged yet?"

He growled at her that if it had he wouldn't still be sprawled underneath her flipping pram, would he? He wasn't doing it for his health. He felt a proper fool, and hoped no one from school would happen to go past and see him. If this got around people could be funny about it and he wouldn't blame them. If it had been somebody else under a pram in the main street he would have been funny about it himself. He pulled savagely at the stubborn brake and the pram almost heeled over. The Kid, sensing disaster, started to whine.

"Be quick! The Oldies are coming!"

Too late, they had come. Like bees round a honey pot they crowded and buzzed and hovered. Miss Sillitoe led them. Away back in history Miss Sillitoe had taught music to most of their mothers. She was very tall and very thin, and from every inch of her where anything could dangle something dangled. Without waiting for an invitation she pushed her head up into the pram's hood, gushing. "Well now! Look who's here! Fancy meeting you! Isn't he a love? Oh, he knows he's a love, doesn't he? Of course he does! He knows! Such a great big fellow! Diddums, then! Aren't you a great big handsome fellow?"

To gain a better view of the Kid Miss Sillitoe with her head still lowered edged round the side of the pram and her long pointed shoe caught in Dan's shopping bag and upset it. Crouched where he was he heard the eggs plopping sickly on the pavement. There was a chance that the cardboard carton would save them, but from the sound of it he didn't think it likely.

The Kid was alarmed by Miss Sillitoe at such close quarters, he whined more urgently. Miss Sillitoe protested archly, asking him what was the matter-watter, then? Her friends crowded closer, sympathetically concerned. Megan was now joggling the pram so fiercely that in self-defence Miss Sillitoe had to withdraw her head from the hood. "That's no way for a gentleman to behave," she scolded the baby as she retreated, straightening her pancaked hat. She waggled two long fingers at the Kid. "Bye bye for now!" All the Oldies waggled their fingers. The lights from the window of the grocery shop made a picture of them. They retreated and drifted up the road, still laughing gently. Bedtime at Eventide was early. Dear Matron would be vexed if they were late.

"Oh stuff it, can't you!" Megan yapped at the baby. "That Miss Sillitoe is crackers, everyone knows she's crackers, especially about babies. It comes of not having any of her own, my Mum says."

Dan said, "I suppose people get like that."

"They're welcome," Megan snapped, "and are you going to take all night over that brake?"

Certainly it was still defeating him. He reached over to retrieve his eggs and set them into the shopping bag. Only one corner oozed, perhaps things weren't as bad as he had feared. But he was tired of Megan nagging, tired of being made to look a fool by a simple piece of mechanism, cross with himself for his inefficiency.

"You were pretty terrible at the rehearsal," he told her. "If you could just have seen yourself! While Gabriel was saying his piece you looked scared into little bits."

"Scared? Well of course I was scared!"

"You weren't! You couldn't have been, not really!"

"I know if I was scared or not."

"But it was only Pete."

Megan said, "If the play is real it isn't Pete, it's the Angel Gabriel. And I'd bet anybody would be scared of the Angel Gabriel."

Dan put his head out from the pram's flank and studied her with a mixture of curiosity and pity. "You're scared of a lot of things, aren't you?"

She flattened her hair back and said, "Everybody gets

scared sometimes and it isn't any business of yours. Anyhow, you needn't talk about the rehearsal. Mr Bingham didn't think you were all that marvellous, and all you had to do was to tag along behind Roger and copy what he was doing."

This stung as it was intended to do. Comparisons with Roger always stung. Dan gave the wire of the brake an extra yank and at last it sprang free. He got up straightening his stiff neck and knees and elbows. "There you are. There's your beastly brake!"

"And about time," she acknowledged ungraciously, and he was just ready to make his escape, when a long polished hand came down on his shoulder and another hand settled on the pram, anchoring them both.

"Well met by street lamp!" They both knew who that was without having to look—Mr Jason Jonson, the actor chappie, who flapped around the streets in a big cloak and a broad-brimmed hat. His long hair, curling on to his shoulders, would have been madly daring on any of the prefects, but it was quite wrong, almost silly, with his old Julius Caesar face. At his age he should have kept to a short back and sides. Mr Jonson had moved into rooms above the Post Office when Mr Everard vacated them. Mrs Hutchin, who cleaned for him to oblige, told Dan's mother that the piano which used to be piled high with Gospel choruses was now packed tight with framed photographs of actors and actresses. Across the corners of the photographs all sorts of loving messages had been scrawled by these famous people who were obviously Mr Jason Jonson's friends. "You only have to look at him to know he's been somebody," the town said. When he stopped in the street to say, "Good morning," people felt as if they ought to clap. He never just talked, he delivered words. Occasionally he read poetry to the Ladies' Meetings. They said just the sound of it made them feel good.

Dan tried to wriggle free and nip off, but Mr Jason Jonson held him tightly. "I've been wanting the chance of a word with you for some time, young man."

"A word with me?"

"The very same. I didn't suspect that you were a fellow Thespian."

"A what?" Dan goggled. This was the first he'd heard of it.

"That evening in the summer, at the Talent Spotting Contest on the pier—now that was a performance. I was proud of you, lad—proud!"

"Oh—that. I didn't know you were there."

"Of course I was there. I made it my business to be there. Beginners on the way up the ladder deserve all the interest and encouragement they can get from those of us who are established in the profession. Young fresh talent, that's what I like to see. Eager—un-spoiled——"

"I made a proper mess of it," Dan growled. He could see that Megan's ears were cocked. It was a pity she had to hear about this.

"You spoke from here," Mr Jason Jonson declared, laying his hand on his heart. "That's where the words ought to come from."

"I wasn't any good. You know they didn't like it."

Mr Jason Jonson's snort blew all unresponsive audiences to Timbuctoo. "Perhaps you didn't quite carry your listeners all the way with you."

"You can say that again." Dan felt a trifle comforted. It was wonderful what saying it like that could do.

"It happens to the best of us, lad. The most sublime of words can fail—anyone who has trod the boards will tell you that. But wait. Just you wait. A time will come, lad, when suddenly—and don't ask me when or why—those words come alive, have being and authority, and you find yourself building bridges with them, out to the people on the other side of the footlights." He spoke with confidence now, he knew what he was talking about, he had used those words and built those bridges. "I remember once Sir Basil said to me—'Jay Jay old boy'—they all called me Jay Jay——"

But the Kid didn't want to hear about Jay Jay or Sir Basil. From the hood's dark recesses he opened up a full-throated yell. "Zounds, he's got lungs!" Mr Jason Jonson said, stretching a finger out to chuck the Kid under his bad-tempered chin and pulling it in again in case he got bitten.

"We're doing a play at school for Christmas," Megan told him, trying to draw his attention away from the baby. "Dan and I are both in it."

"You are? Splendid, splendid! That's what I like to hear. And if I can be of any help, any trifling piece of advice, a matter of interpretation or of delivery perhaps, well, you know you only have to ask. Drop in on me any time, don't hesitate, for a venture like that I can always find the time."

They thanked him. He asked what the play was. "A

Nativity Play," they told him, feeling a little foolish because he would think this was kids' stuff, not anything with style and drama.

They were surprised when the old actor's eyes grew serious and steady. He drew himself up to his full height, removed his hat and held it. He stood between lamplight and shoplight, gravely and splendidly dignified. "You have chosen the greatest theme of all time," he said, and then replaced his hat and went striding up towards the Post Office, where all the photographs of his famous friends were waiting for him.

They stared after him. "Did you hear what he said?"

"He's batty, batty as they come."

"Maybe we will get it right—the play I mean.' Megan's voice sounded anxious, as if it had begun to matter.

"Not a hope," Dan told her, because it would be inconvenient to the rest of them if anyone got ideas like this, "and remember what I said about Pete. You don't have to be scared."

She nodded doubtfully and pulled the pram round, ready to head for home.

"Hi, Megan! Hold on a minute!"

"What is it?"

"I just wondered." He turned to the shop window, inspecting the tins of soup so that he needn't see her face. "Philip—was he scared of things?"

She said, "I expect so," and was off down the street with the pram at full speed, the turning wheels making bright circles as they passed through each of the pools of light thrown from the windows of the shops.

Chapter Four

It was on the day of the fifth rehearsal that the angels decided unanimously they wouldn't turn up. Instead they retired to the Girls' Cloakroom and waited until they saw Fred going past, then they whistled at him and told him their tidings, and that he could pass the news on to Mr Bingham.

Poor peaceable Fred! He was scandalized by this behaviour. He turned red and stammered, "But you've got to come! You know Mr Bingham said——"

They were calm but firm. "Never you mind what he said. We told you. We've made up our minds. We aren't coming."

"What'll I say to him?" Fred inquired uneasily.

"Tell him, that's all. Tell him what we said."

"I can't."

"Why not?"

"He'll want to know why."

"If he asks you can say we've decided to have a sit-in."

Fred's eyes were out on stalks. "A sit-in? But why?"

They sniffed. "That's our business. If Mr Bingham wants to find out why let him ask Sir Roger."

"Roger? What's Roger got to do with it?"

"Oh, go on, you'll be late," they scolded. They were tired of his standing there gulping reproachfully at them like a frog. He saw that they meant it. They had brought their knitting. No one, certainly not Fred, stood a chance of arguing successfully through the door of the Girls' Cloakroom with a gaggle of knitting angels.

Fred gave this news to the others before Mr Bingham arrived. Dan rounded on Roger accusingly. "They've gone broody and it's your fault!"

"My fault?" Roger's eyebrows pushed all responsibility sky high.

"Oh, wrap it up. You remember what you did the first day they tried on their wings!"

"Me?"

"You made 'puck puck' noises and wanted to know whether they were free range or battery. That's what they're on about. You are a nit!"

Roger protested that girls were a lot of silly clucks anyway and ought to be able to take a joke.

"That was a bit much, all the same. You'd better nip along before Mr Bingham comes, and tell them you're sorry. Go on!"

So Roger, who wasn't accustomed to taking orders from Dan, trailed off crossly to make apologetic noises through the door of the Girls' Cloakroom while the rest of them stood at the end of the corridor watching, and enjoyed his embarrassment. The angels went on purling and plaining as briskly as ever until they were satisfied that his apology was loud enough and then they furled up their wool and made it to the classroom just in time.

This didn't mean that any of the actors had become madly keen about the play. But they were resigned to the idea and anxious now to get it performed with the least possible fuss and bother. Dan had passed Mr Jason Jonson's comment around the class, and perhaps this had helped. "The greatest theme of all time." If a recognized celebrity like Jason Jonson had said that then the play deserved their respect. They were prepared to go through with it politely and efficiently, and everyone had learned his or her part. Rehearsals had continued to be flat but maybe that was the safest way for them to be. They kept a wary eye on Fred, with his record of annual salvation, assuring him that Megan had been right when she'd said that all Joseph did was stand at the back. No one wanted anyone else's enthusiasm to spread. At every rehearsal a little less of Mr Bingham's bounce and self-confidence was evident.

Meanwhile the music corridor was loud with carols, and the pastoral symphony, that smooth moonlit part of the music from Handel's *Messiah* which the music master had arranged for the recorders. All kinds of argument and debate were rolling about, especially in the Art Room. What was the most satisfactory way of fastening on a halo? Miss Hunt favoured a wired head-piece, Annette and the Sob Sisters said they would be happier with elastic. How long were wings and what shape should they be? Beards for all three kings or only a beard for Melchior? What did frankincense look like when you met it, and what sort of an object did you use

58

to carry it about, a box or a jug? And while you were on the subject did anybody know anything about myrrh? Gold? Gold was easy, someone's aunt had a smashing brass cigarette box which would be just the job.

"Tell your father, Dan, we shall want seven crooks for the shepherds," Mr Bingham had said, "and about four feet long would be ideal." Dan had taken this message home but there was no sign that his father had heard what he said.

Meanwhile Miss Hunt was collecting curtains, bed-spreads and dressing-gowns from all her friends and relations. Every lunch-hour the Holy Family, the Kings and the shepherds were draped and redraped, swathed and measured, and inspected by Mr Bingham. "It is *so* important to have every detail right," Miss Hunt insisted, blinking her large pale eyes critically at her handiwork and sticking in pins.

On the day of the fourth rehearsal the girls had brought their dolls to school, so that a selection from them could be made. Of course they were too old now to play with dolls, but they had hunted for past darlings through the top shelves of their toy cupboards and un-peeled them from their tissue paper and shaken out the frills. They cooed and became sentimental. The class-room was like a toyshop, the boys didn't know where to look and felt the tips of their ears growing red. The ranks of china invaders opened their eyes and closed them and said "Mamma!"

After much discussion, Miss Hunt cooing with the best of them, a final choice was made. It was fat Margie's

59

doll. Mary was furnished with it as a substitute for the rolled-up blazer. Somehow this should have made a difference to her but it didn't. The doll, lifelike and life-size as it was, was no more real when Megan was holding it than the rolled-up blazer had been. "Tell your father we'll be glad to have those crooks he's making for us at the next rehearsal, will you, Dan?" Mr. Bingham had said.

Dan, scuffing his way unhappily home that evening, wished that the dry tide of autumn leaves on the road had been more substantial and made more satisfying stuff for kicking. There was no comfort this evening from the sucking sound of a full tide at the sea wall or from the wing of light spread out across the water from the lighthouse. Dan had taught himself to calculate the intervals between these flashes to the hair's breadth of a split second and he prided himself on this achievement. Sometimes he closed his eyes, and as he opened them again said, "Now!" and knew that the beam from the lighthouse would answer him obediently. He could do the same with the town clock, estimating the moments of silence between the striking of the four quarters and the deep bell that counted the hours. And lying in bed at night listening to the oncoming train he could fore-tell exactly when it would whistle. To know these things and be right about them gave him a sense of pleasure, almost as if he owned them. But this evening he made no claim to the lighthouse, he hardly saw it. He spotted Roger farther down the road and slowed his pace so that he needn't catch up. Did he imagine it, or had Roger spotted him and quickened his own pace?

Then, as the sea-front curved, he lost sight of Roger and when he expected to see him again found he had disappeared. This was odd. Where had he gone? The chip shop had closed. He must have moved fast to be out of sight already.

What was Dan going to say to his father anyway? The shepherds, at the last rehearsal, had had to make do with bamboo canes from the potting shed to serve them as crooks. Dan knew he was going to look pretty silly if Dad didn't come up with the goods soon. He tried to frame sentences that he could say to his father this evening, sentences that would sound easy and casual (of course Dad was going to supply crooks to the shepherds) and yet would let him know that the matter was urgent. The words became tangled in his unhappy mind. Whose side was he on, anyway? Did he have to champion Dad against Mr Bingham? What reasons could he give? It was his Dad's business, wasn't it, if he hadn't been in his workshop since the day of Philip Lloyd's accident?

He was now passing in front of Eventide Home. The lights in the large drawing-room were lit but the curtains had not yet been drawn across the windows. The Oldies sat in their appointed armchairs, solid and separate as islands. They looked peaceful. Dan envied them their peace, their freedom from the rival demands of family loyalties and personal irritations. They didn't get themselves involved in long inward debates as to what they should say and whose side they were on. Their loneliness made all that unnecessary. They were lucky.

He noticed that the pair of large ornamental flower

61

urns which sat on each side of the hall door of Eventide had been tipped over and lay beside a heap of spilled earth and scattered petals. One of the urns was broken. The Wreckers had made a thorough job of them last night. It must have been easy enough, hardly worth putting on their masks for. By the time the crash had brought anybody to the windows of Eventide the trespassers would have been out of sight. They were clever, the Wreckers. They never left enough evidence to prove their identity.

He was still chewing his own problems when he turned the next corner, and so had forgotten to protect himself against the daily disappointment, and when he saw the lighted window of the shop and the square of yellow light thrown from it on to the road it took him completely by surprise, and made him catch his breath. He stopped short, letting the joyful sight fill him through, from his heels to the crown of his head. The light was there! Things were going to be all right, after all. Dad was in his workshop and all was right with the world. The shepherds would have magnificent crooks and the smile would be wiped off Roger's face. Things at home would be the way they used to be. Glory be! Goodwill and glory flowed in him as he moved forward and pushed the door of the shop open and stepped inside.

Only it wasn't Dad. It was his mother. She had her back to him and didn't hear him coming in, so that he stood watching her and tried not to drown in the tide of his own fierce disappointment. What business had she there? This was Dad's place, she never came into the shop. And what was she doing? Whatever it was it would be unwelcome, and she looked silly, for she must have come straight from her duties at the Hotel and was still wearing her black shiny dress with the white cuffs and the frilly apron. Dan never liked her in those clothes. It was the uniform of the pleasant slave who smiled and said of course sir, and indeed it wouldn't be any trouble madam, and be sure you give me a handsome tip for playing this game with you, for allowing you to be the Big People.

"You know he doesn't like you to touch his things."

She turned round and saw him. "Dan!"

"If you mess his tools about he won't know where they are."

She put the tools she was holding on to the bench again, almost as if she were afraid of them. He could see now that she had been tidying up. The glass panes of the window shone. The small mountain of shavings from below the lathe had been scooped into a corner. Her apron was smeared with grease and cobwebs.

"What do you think you're doing, anyway?"

"That's no way for you to speak, Dan!"

"But what are you doing?" It was easy to say impossible things to her if he shouted them. If he stopped shouting and remembered who she was he would be struck dumb.

"I'm only tidying up a little," she said, as if she knew she had no business there.

"He doesn't want it like that. The way it is he knows just where he can lay his hand on anything. If you start mucking it around——"

"You know I hate to see dirt."

"You don't have to see it if you stay out of here." It wasn't his mother he was talking to. If it had been his mother he couldn't have said these things, or if he had said them she would have silenced him by her sharp scandalized anger, and he would have been a little boy again, the way he always was when his mother was angry. He would have been sorry and ashamed and in need of her forgiveness before the world could go on. But he didn't need anything from her now because this wasn't his mother.

"Don't you get enough cleaning to do at home? You're always scrubbing and dusting and wiping and tidying and polishing. Nothing's ever right until you've cleaned it. Things being clean is more important than being happy or comfortable. That's what you're like— like Baboushka!"

His mother stared at him. "Like who?"

"Like Baboushka. Don't you know who Baboushka was?" Her ignorance made him feel grander than ever.

"Who was she?"

"There's a story about her. She was a housewife, the kind that never had any visitors because they'd mess the house about. Only one night she did have visitors. It was the Three Kings on their way to Bethlehem, and they told her why they were going there and showed her the star in the sky, and asked if they could stay in her house overnight."

"Did she say they could?"

"Yes, if they wiped their feet and didn't drop cigarette ash around."

"Now you're being silly."

"All right, if you don't want to know."

"I do want to know. Go on."

"In the morning the Kings asked Baboushka if she'd like to go with them to Bethlehem, and she said she would, only——"

"Only what?"

"What do you think? Of course she would have to straighten the place up after them, wouldn't she? She couldn't just walk out and shut the door on the house the way it was."

"So what did she do?"

"She told the Kings to go on ahead, and as soon as she had tidied up and left everything ready and clean to come back to, she would follow them."

"And did she?"

"She couldn't. She was busy cleaning all day, and the next evening when she looked for the star she couldn't see it. She didn't know which was the way to Bethlehem. So she missed it all."

His mother's face had turned red and she wasn't looking at him any more, but was turning one of Dad's screwdrivers over and over in her hand, not seeing it.

"What did you say her name was?"

"Baboushka. We had it in school."

He felt his power to be angry seeping out of him. He hoped she would be angry now. That would put things right. That would be easier than if he had to feel sorry for her. He would rather feel sorry for himself and he could do that if she was angry.

"I thought your father might have more heart in the

place when he comes back to it if it was tidied up a bit," she said.

This made it possible for him to ask, "When is he coming back to it, Mum?"

She was prodding with the screwdriver into the soft place in the palm of her hand, making marks there and watching them disappear.

"I thought he was starting this morning. He went out of the house, not saying anything, but I watched and he turned up the hill instead, towards the woods."

"And then?"

"When I came back from the shops he was home before me."

"Where had he been?"

"Dan—you know I couldn't ask."

He'd let her off that if she'd answer his next question. "What keeps him from coming back, Mum?" Even if she didn't answer it was an indulgence to be able to ask.

"You know what keeps him, Dan."

"Because of the accident. Because of what happened to Philip Lloyd."

His mother nodded.

"But Dad had fixed those brakes when he was overhauling Philip's bike the week before. He knew there wasn't anything wrong with them."

"People can make mistakes."

"Not that kind of a mistake. Not Dad."

She twisted the edge of her apron between her fingers.

"You're getting oil on yourself," he told her and she let the frills go, smoothing them down without looking. "There must have been something else," he said.

66

"It was the people in the town, your father's friends. As soon as word got about——"

"They thought it was Dad's fault, you mean?"

"Nobody said it was. Nobody said it wasn't. Not one. Not one of them. Your father has worked in this town all his life, they know the class of work he does and the pride he takes in it. Not one of them spoke up. Not one said it couldn't possibly have been your father's fault."

So that was it! His father wasn't tormented by the thought of what he might have done to Philip Lloyd, he was offended with his friends for believing that he could have made a mistake. It was Dad's pride as much as Philip's back that had been hurt. Dan would almost have preferred that his father had been willing to take the blame for faulty brakes.

"It's himself he's sorry for, not because Philip may be a cripple!" he accused.

"You be quiet! What can you know about it, a child like you?"

This was the way she ought to talk and he was glad. It made him feel a child again straight away. It put him back in the box where he belonged. He felt his eyes sting and was afraid he was going to cry.

"I'm sorry! I'm sorry!"

She set the screwdriver down and stretched a hand out for his shoulder. "That's all right, Dan. All right now. I know. It was just that you didn't understand."

If Mum said he didn't understand then it must be true and he needn't try. When you were a child you were excused. She had said so. He and his mother were now both back where they belonged. She pushed her hair off her forehead and smiled at him. "It makes it worse for your father with things going so well for your Uncle Bill."

"I never thought about that."

"It's only natural, between brothers. If you'd had a brother yourself you'd understand. Your uncle could never use his hands the way your father can, but he has a good head for business, he's making a big name for himself in the city, everyone knows that, or if they don't your Aunt Florence soon tells them."

It was exciting to be invited to criticize Aunt Florence.

"She does go on a bit, doesn't she?"

"You shouldn't say that. She's had a hard enough time."

"Hard?" He laughed.

"It's true, your uncle was never the easiest of men."

Uncle Bill had always seemed easy, a bit too easy, too smooth, but useful sometimes for extra cash if you allowed yourself to take it.

His mother stirred the sawdust on the bench with her finger, tracing letters in it. "When they were younger the two brothers were always trying to get even with each other. If one had a new car the other had to have one the same. They both were after the same girl——"

He loved her fiercely and said, "I'm glad it was Dad who got you."

She scooped the sawdust off the bench on to the floor and blew on her hand. "It was Florence they both wanted."

He wished she hadn't said that, even if it was true. He

hated what she had said as much as he hated her servant's uniform. It rocked the foundations of everything he knew to be permanent, making an accident of the family group and of himself. Instead of reaching back into an unalterable inheritance of history he was only himself, Dan Agnew, because his Aunt Florence had preferred Uncle Bill.

"Then that's why he's always on at me to do better than Roger," he said. He didn't need to ask.

There wasn't anything more that they could say to each other. If she'd been angry with him and shouted he would have welcomed it. But she said, "You get on home. I'll lock up here when I'm finished," and he let himself out of the shop into the darkening road where the patch from the lighted shop window now burned like gold. For some reason that he knew to be unreasonable he was careful not to step into the square of light. It had become necessary to avoid it. But instead of going home he turned back again in the direction of the sea-front. He couldn't be in the same room as his father and pretend that nothing had changed. He needed time to think, to get things sorted out. He was angry with his mother because it was her fault that he felt like this. She shouldn't have told him these things. What business had she telling things that should be private to a child like him? Grown-ups were the people who had to deal with such affairs. They knew the words and the explanations and the proper way to feel.

The sea-front was deserted except for a whistling errand boy who was pushing newspapers into letter-boxes. Dan trudged as far as the limit of the sea wall, where a promontory of rough rock pushed out into the water and the road turned inland. Here he halted. The sides of the promontory fell in steep cliffs to the sea. The tide had just turned but was still pounding the base of the cliff, throwing up plumes of spray before the water ran steeply into the oncoming waves. Dan hauled himself on to the buttress where the sea wall ended, and lay looking down, enjoying the violence of the water; there was a kind of honesty about it which he admired and envied. The beam of the lighthouse held each wave for a frozen moment before it swept past. It was a battle between the light and the water. The water won every time.

There was someone out there on the headland! Dan had to wait for the next sweep of the lighthouse before he could be sure. Yes, someone was there, more than one person. On the skyline at the top of the cliff humped shapes that could only be people were huddled together. Five or six of them, perhaps. Fools! Didn't they know it wasn't safe out there, there were enough barbed wire and notices about to warn off the summer visitors, anybody belonging to the town had more sense. It was asking for trouble to go out there any time, let alone in the dark. The sides of the rock ran down straight into the water at high tide, only a few bunches of tough grass could find a home in the lightly scarred surface. If anyone fell from the top—Dan's eye was forced down the cliff face, as if by acknowledging the danger he could protect those stupid idiots from it. And then, as the lighthouse beam crossed over the cliff again, his stomach lurched. Someone was there on the rock face, flattened against it, fingers and toes fighting for purchase, moving slowly down towards the water. It was a boy, a small boy. Once when a jutting ledge allowed him to pause he lifted his face and looked up to the watchers from the cliff top as if asking permission to return, but they waved him on, and he continued his slow hazardous journey.

Dan wanted to yell, but what good could yelling do? The rough wind and the sound of the waves would smother any noise he made. He wanted to stop looking but this too was impossible. He had to share what was going on, just as the watchers from the cliff top were sharing it. He hated the excitement and sense of power that he knew they were feeling and that he could now feel in himself. Once the figure on the cliff face fumbled his hold and snatched desperately for another one, and Dan's fingers clawed painfully at the stones of the wall beneath him.

The climber had now reached the bottom of the cliff and was standing where the confusion of breaking water sucked over his feet and rose waist-high round him before it was pulled sharply back again. He stood there while seven waves came and went round his body. Any of them could have carried him back with it. He rocked, almost stumbled, but stood his ground. At the top of the cliff the raised arms of the watchers counted out the seven waves. Then they signalled permission for the climber to return, and he began to go up again the way he had come down. Dan shared with him every movement, every indecision, every triumph. At last the climber's fingers groped for and found the springy grass that grew at the top of the cliff. Hands from the watching group came out to pull him up and into safety. They stood up, thumping him and calling congratulations. One of the group was taller than the others.

Now the boys were coming back off the headland, towards the road. Dan lay where he was, flat as a fly against the stonework, hoping they wouldn't spot him. They climbed the sea wall a few hundred yards from him and dropped into the road. They were too full of excitement and the sense of danger past to have noticed him, and they went off towards the town, chattering like sparrows. Dan identified the taller figure among them. It was Roger. He knew that he had expected it to be Roger.

The climber followed them, keeping his distance. The trailing finger of the lighthouse showed Dan who it was—the kid Ronnie Simpson, Roger's page. He was trotting in the direction of his home and crying, crying like a baby, with not enough grace or shame to try to stop it—just crying. Water ran out of his clothes. His teeth were chattering.

Dan slithered off the wall and caught up with Ronnie. "Hi there!"

He didn't think the kid saw him. He caught hold of him by the elbow and jerked him round so that he had to slow down and listen. "What else did Roger tell you you had to do? What sort of things does he make the others do? Go on—I want to know. What about Philip Lloyd? Tell me about him!"

But the kid just stared at him as if he didn't hear and twisted out of his grasp and ran up the road, still crying.

 *Chapter Five*

Annette favoured Mr Bingham's idea of a visit by the whole cast to the Art Gallery in the city, though most of the rest of them were far from keen.

"It's bound to be a terrific help to us at the next rehearsal," she declared to her companion angels, "like Mr Bingham says. I mean we'll feel much more real once we've seen ourselves in all those famous pictures."

Fat Margie grumbled that she didn't see why. The less real Margie felt the better it pleased her. She made it her regular practice to slither past mirrors and to avoid looking into any shiny surfaces which might reflect her. To herself, looking down, she seemed quite a reasonable size. Mirrors were cheats, they just spread her out, like butter on a slice of bread.

Annette doted on mirrors. They told her things about herself that she longed for other people to tell her. Among the Nativity pictures in the Art Gallery she knew she was bound to discover an angel—the chief angel of course, the one with the solo part—who would look out at her with her own eyes. "Like this," the angel in the picture would tell her. "Here you are! Like this!" The rest of the class would notice. "There's Annette!" they would say, nudging. "There! Look!"

Annette looked forward to finding herself in the Art Gallery. Recently she had spent a great deal of her time trying to find herself; the pages of her mother's glossy magazines said that this was important. "Know your Type!" they insisted. There were any number of types —the Sporty type, the Girl-Next-Door type, the Little-Girl-Lost type, the Hard-to-Get, the Fragile, the Mysterious. Annette didn't think she fitted into the same type for two days running. A lot depended on what clothes you were wearing and who you were with and what the day was like. It was no good asking the other girls about yourself, they were much too keen for you to tell them what type you thought they were. And she felt awkward about asking Mum, though Mum, of course, would have known.

Recently Annette had come across a page in a magazine which said, "Come to terms with the Real You! Find out Your Own Secrets! Be more Fully yourself! Use TRUE ALLURE—specially produced for you—and watch your true personality shine through!" She had cut out the coupon and sent it with the twenty pence in stamps and a stamped addressed envelope to the required address, and waited. Last Wednesday the postman had brought her a small package which yielded an even smaller tube of TRUE ALLURE, and she had used it with faith and hope every night, reading the instructions over carefully. She tried to persuade herself that there was a difference, but it wasn't a difference that she could actually feel or

74

that anyone else had noticed. Nothing seemed to be shining through after all, not even a flicker. Once Mum had asked if she'd been crying and that was all. And now the tube was nearly empty. She knew she ought to feel established and fulfilled and sure of her type by this time if the stuff was any good. So often things that ought to have been lovely turned out like this.

Mr Bingham had decided that a visit to the Art Gallery might do for his actors what Annette's sample had failed to do for her. "You just need to see yourselves in your parts, that's all you need," he declared, and booked a coach to take them. This meant missing a rehearsal so they went quietly enough. Miss Hunt had come with them, and had brought her sketch book. "The Old Masters!" she purred. "We're bound to come back with a hatful of new ideas!"

"I feel quite excited about this, don't you?" Annette asked Dan who was sharing a seat in the bus with her.

"No," he said.

It was a pity he felt like that. Annette knew that Dan hadn't sat down beside her because he wanted to, but that he had been standing at the entrance to the bus checking the names for Mr Bingham, and when it was time for him to take his seat the only one that was vacant was next to Annette. He could have shifted one of the kids, but he didn't. He sat down beside Annette. She didn't suppose he'd ever sat next to a girl in a bus before.

Annette wished he would say something. If the others noticed him talking to her they would think he had chosen to sit beside her, and she would like them to think this. She might even persuade herself that TRUE ALLURE was working. But anyone could tell by the way Dan was sitting, all humped up and staring straight ahead, that he'd much rather have been sitting with the other boys at the back. Perhaps if she talked to him he would talk.

"What did you think of our haloes when we tried them on the other day?"

Dan sniffed and rubbed his hand across his nose. He said the haloes were all right, he supposed. His hands were square and rough with short nails and freckles along the back. Annette spread her own small hands on her lap and hoped he noticed the difference. 'The Fragile'—was that perhaps her type?

"Did you really like them?"

"Like what?"

"What I was asking—our haloes."

"They were all right."

"Joe said they were like little gold plates stuck on. He would say that. You didn't think they were like that, did you?"

"I told you."

"I mean you'd have known what they were supposed to be all right?"

Boys are shy. All the glossy magazines were sure about this. Boys find it harder to talk than girls do. But persevere. Be natural. Chat away about anything. Don't try to be clever or talk about something you don't understand. Ask questions. Most boys like to be invited to give their opinions.

"Go on," she invited him, "what did yo[u] really looked like?"

"Like angels, I suppose," he growled, "like you were meant to look."

She would wring a compliment out of him if it killed her. "Heavenly, you mean?"

"I suppose so."

That was as much as she was going to get. But it was something. It was something that she could write down in her diary this evening. "Dan Agnew sat next to me in the bus going to the Art Gallery and told me that I looked heavenly when I was dressed up as an angel." She decided that she could write that down without cheating. Life wasn't easy, you had to make the best of it. She would tell the other angels what Dan had said.

"I thought you looked marvellous," she told him, "all the girls were saying how marvellous you were. That Chinese coat of Mr Anstruther's——"

"His dressing-gown——"

"It's a beauty."

"Everybody'll know it's a dressing-gown."

"We'll all feel better," she comforted him, "when we have got our slap on."

She heard his jaw drop. "Our *what*?" He had to ask it. The question was jerked out of him.

"Our slap. Don't you know? That's what real theatre people call their make-up." She felt delightfully superior, and hoped some of the girls were listening.

"Who told you?"

She wished he would turn round a little to show the

77

others what an interesting conversation they were having, but he never budged, just allowed words to escape sideways at her out of the corner of his mouth.

"Mr Jason Jonson, he told me. He's such a fascinating man, don't you think? It's wonderful to talk to a real celebrity like he is. You can say anything to him, he's so understanding. He's very interested in our play, you know. He's been asking me about it. He's sure we'll feel quite different with our slap on. And on the night, with the audience all there, when the drapes go up——" She waited for him to ask her what "the drapes" were but he didn't. It was no use. She fumbled in her pocket until she found a peppermint, and decided to console herself with this. It would last longer if she didn't talk. They travelled the rest of the way in silence.

Mr Bingham assembled his cast on the steps of the Art Gallery. "Now you know what you've come for, don't you?" he inquired briskly. Miss Hunt, poised pink-faced across her sketch-book, nodded. The rest of them avoided his eye. Someone had said Mr Bingham was going to stand them ices all round on the way home. "In this building," Mr Bingham continued, jerking his head towards the Gallery, "you will discover portraits of yourselves. I want you to study them. You will learn more from these pictures than I could ever tell you. Study them slowly, one at a time and no pushing. Don't hurry, look at each picture as long as you want to look. Think of the great men who painted them. Notice the details—even small things can become important. If you want to talk, talk quietly. No fooling about. Some of these pictures are hundreds of years old but as true today as they were on the day they were painted. Now get along, up the stairs and the second door on the left. Remember we don't want any funny business. See if you can find what we've come for."

They entered the large marble-floored entrance hall and mounted the stairs, feeling self-conscious and unexpectedly important.

The second door on the left, Mr Bingham had told them. They reached it and went in warily, treading as if they were entering Church.

It was like stepping full tilt into a crowd of giants who pushed and jostled for their attention. The walls of the gallery were filled solid with pictures from floor to ceiling. There were no windows, all the light came from glass panes overhead. It seemed as if there was plenty of light but very little living air, and no hint at all of the world outside. The giants in the pictures closed the children in, they were trapped by them. They hadn't expected to feel like this.

At first it was difficult to look only at one picture at a time, but slowly characters and places sorted themselves out and were identified. But there were mistakes in these pictures. They looked more closely—yes, plenty of mistakes. To protect themselves against too much grandeur and solemnity the children spotted these mistakes joyfully and told each other about them. "Just take a look," Joe said to the shepherd who was standing beside him, "curious sort of a stable, if you ask me. Shiny pillars and roses and all that marble. And I don't think much of that for a manger. Whoever painted that hadn't ever been inside a stable in his life."

"Anyway, it was supposed to be in the bleak mid-winter, wasn't it?"

"According to Mr Bingham that might be just a tradition. Nobody is sure that it did happen in the winter after all."

"Of course Christmas is winter. Think of the rein-deer!"

"Reindeers are only kid's stuff," Joe said witheringly, and his companion wilted. He should have remembered of course that Father Christmas is a man dressed up and snow is made from cotton wool. "You'd think some-body would have known what time of year it was all the same," he complained, "but the roses are very good. You'd almost think they were real."

"I expect that's why he put them in; he could paint roses but he wasn't any good at stables."

"The donkey's all right."

"Too fat." Joe knew about donkeys. "And none of these shepherds are dressed up in striped bedspreads the way Miss Hunt has got us."

"Shepherds are always stripey in the Bible."

"Not around here they aren't." He moved on to look for shepherds who were stripey.

"Would she really have been wearing all that jewel-lery?" one of the angels was asking Megan. "I mean, would she have had any to wear? Joseph was just a carpenter. They were poor. And fancy wearing pearls in a stable!"

Megan moved quickly to another picture. Even if

she'd had the pearls and worn them, that wasn't what she'd have looked like, so tidy, so beautiful, so serene, after she'd spent the night lying on straw giving birth to a baby. Megan knew. She had carried tea up to her Mum after the last two babies had been born. But moving to another picture didn't help, nor did the picture beyond. Picture after picture showed Mary with not a fold of her blue mantle creased or crooked, and her hair as if she'd just stepped out of a Beauty Salon, always a different face but always that unassailable composure. Mum never looked like that.

"They're not as big as that just after they've been born, are they?"

"No."

The child in this picture was sitting upright and raising an instructive finger to the Wise Men.

"He's very well painted."

All the babies were well painted, they were all beautiful, but Margie's doll had been just as real.

Poor Fred was pacing from one picture to the next, anxious to find himself figuring prominently in the important role of Joseph. But every picture proved that the girls had been right. Joseph was always standing at the back. Indeed in one picture he wasn't even standing, he was stretched out asleep on the stable floor, completely missing the entry of the three Kings with their gifts. Fred moved away quickly in case someone else would notice and want to be funny.

Annette was disappointed in the angels, all with the same face, cut to the same design as if they were wearing uniform, all looking so smug and so good. Their haloes, she thought, did look like little gold plates, no matter what Dan Agnew had said. And there was nothing to show who was Chief Angel. Surely there should have been something, another inch of feather perhaps, an extra star?

Dan had been careful to keep clear of Roger and Sid so that he could make a tour of the pictures on his own and choose the one in which Melchior showed up to the best advantage. "There I am. That's Melchior." But there wasn't one that he wanted to choose. It was unfair. In every picture Caspar and Baltazar appeared as fine regal figures, handsome and upstanding; even without their crowns you would have known that they were kings, even when they knelt you would have known. He saw Roger and Sid admiring themselves, striking the same pose, asking each other, "How's that?" Oh, they were enjoying themselves, putting on inches with every picture. Dan's envy burned. In all the pictures Melchior was a frail old man, you could see that the hands holding his gift were shaky, you knew he'd have trouble getting up off the stable floor with knees as stiff as his knees were. It must have been an elderly docile kind of camel that had brought this man on the long miles to Bethlehem, an old man's mount. Dan had imagined himself full of wisdom and majesty astride the fleetest animal in his kingdom, storming over the eastern plains while the light of the star struck points of brilliance from the jewels in his crown. But Melchior wasn't like that. He was an old man creeping painfully forward to lay a gift in front of a sleeping child.

Miss Hunt was busy. She had crouched down beside a picture with her sketching pad open on her knee, and was copying the drapery of Mary's cloak, fold for fold, as if by faithfully reproducing it at the next rehearsal she could change Megan into Mary. "We'll get it right, you'll see," she smiled encouragingly at Megan, but Megan pretended she hadn't heard, and moved scowling towards the door.

They were all drifting to the door, they had seen as much as they wanted to see and were anxious to get away. The majesty of the pictures made them restless and uneasy. The mistakes in them didn't really matter. In spite of mistakes these pictures were noble and true. Though they were all different each of them was true. And not one of them had anything to do with a school Nativity play, with dressing up and pretending, with cardboard haloes or striped bedspreads or a brass cigarette box that looked like gold. They came downstairs feeling like a lot of kids who have been caught playing a nursery game which they should have grown out of long ago. Anyway, you didn't play games with giants. They were glad to see the outside world again, and hear the stir of the city street.

The coach to take them back to school hadn't yet arrived. "Any time now," Mr Bingham said and steered them into the Reference Library to wait. "Plenty here to interest you."

"Take a look around," the friendly librarian invited them, and they turned their attention gratefully to books. There was safety in facts.

Annette had spotted a book called *The Actors' and*

Entertainers' Who's Who, and now itched to get at it. The names on these pages would be the names of people who had arrived, the Celebrities. Her name would be in this book one day.

"Interested in the stage, are you?" the friendly librarian inquired. How kind of him to want to know.

"Oh I am. Very."

"Intending to make a career of it yourself, perhaps?"

"Oh I'd like to." She was glad she had risked putting on some eyeshadow and that Miss Hunt hadn't spotted it.

"Acting's in the family, is it?"

"Well—no. But I've got friends."

"Anybody you'd specially like to look up? It's all here." He slapped the covers of *The Actors' and Entertainers' Who's Who*. "Professional name, real name, date and place of birth, details of training, principal roles played——"

"You could look up Mr Jason Jonson if you like," she said, "he's a great friend of mine," and waited for him to be impressed.

"Right." The man flicked over the pages and arrived at "J". "Jason—what name did you say?"

"Jason Jonson." She was disappointed that he had to be told.

"Johnstone or Johnson?" the man inquired. "With a 't' in the middle, with an 'e' at the end or not?"

She spelt it out. "J—o—n—s—o—n. No 'e'. No 't'."

His thumbnail skimmed down the columns. "J—o—n—? You're sure that's the way he spells it?"

"I told you."

"And that's his professional name, the name he uses for acting?"

"Yes." Her stomach sagged, her knees had begun to feel cold and uncertain, but she said firmly, "In the theatre people call him J. J. He's very well known."

The librarian's thumb was still unsuccessful. "Better take a look at the other ways of spelling it, just in case," he decided, turning back.

"It can't be much of a book if it makes mistakes in how people's names are spelt," Annette said. She leaned an insolent elbow on the polished counter and prayed that this man might be confounded.

"No other name, just Jason?"

"Just Jason."

"Not here." He whisked the pages over to the alternative spelling. "Not here either."

She kept her elbow where it was and hoped her face wasn't turning red. "It must be there." She blew on the counter and drew with her finger in the mist that her breath had made.

The man smiled more kindly than ever. "It isn't, my dear. Of course bit part actors don't get a mention, only the regulars, the reasonably established names. I expect your friend is a youngster on his way up, a rising star? Eh? Tell him we'll keep some room for him in the next edition. We'll be seeing his name in lights, will we?"

Plainly this was not her afternoon. It was impossible to tell this kind man the truth. She withdrew her elbow and hunted for her handkerchief. She blew and said, "There must be some mistake."

85

"These things do happen," he agreed, still unbearably pleasant. Of course he was playing her game now so that she wouldn't be altogether flattened by her embarrassment.

Fat Margie had drifted in her direction and wanted to be told what the book was. When it had been explained she asked the librarian to look up Tom Jones and he flicked the pages readily and turned it round for her to read—there was a lot to read about Tom Jones. Annette listened to Margie lapping it up, and mourned privately for her friend, the well-known actor, Mr Jason Jonson. He wasn't a glorious hasbeen after all. If this book was right he'd never even been. The only big thing about him was the way he talked. Could that be true? Could life really be as cruel as that? All those assumed triumphs, that easy sense of being at home with glamour, those trailing clouds of past glories, had he invented them? When Margie had been sated with Tom Jones they wandered out into the hall together and Annette told her what she had discovered, or failed to discover, about Mr Jason Jonson. Maybe it was treachery, but it helped to ease the sting.

"And his name isn't even there!"

Fat Margie was obligingly scandalized. "But it must be!"

"It isn't. All those signed photographs in his room, how do you suppose——?"

Margie knew. "That's easy. You send a stamped addressed envelope."

"Just like that?"

Margie nodded, speechless with indignation, and

Annette felt a little consoled. Now the coach had arrived and Mr Bingham was rounding up the party. "Come along now. No shoving. Be sure you haven't left anything behind. Everyone take the place you had on your way here." They were seated, and ice-creams were handed round. Annette wished she had the strength of will to refuse, but the cold sweetness on her tongue employed and comforted her.

The coach commenced its homeward journey. "That's the Hospital where Philip Lloyd is, did you know?" Annette said as they passed it. She stared at the cliff of glass and concrete, wondering which window Philip looked out of, which patch of sky he saw. She had had her appendix out in that building, and had owned her patch of sky.

The moment she said it she knew it was a mistake. Of course she shouldn't have mentioned Philip Lloyd, not to Dan. Everyone knew that Philip's bicycle had been in Mr Agnew's shop for an overhaul just before the accident, people said perhaps something hadn't been looked at properly, and the brakes could have been wrongly adjusted. The accident might have been Mr Agnew's fault. Now she hadn't a hope of getting a syllable out of Dan all the way home.

"Did you know Philip Lloyd well?"

She was so astounded that she couldn't answer him straight away.

"Well—did you?" he insisted.

"Not really, but sometimes when I was collecting the kids' dinner tickets for Miss Patterson Philip used to talk to me. He used to tell me things."

Dan had twisted round in his seat to look at her. "What sort of things?"

She felt triumphant. So they were going to have a conversation after all. Ideas, like table tennis balls, would fly between them. "Your ice-cream is dripping," she warned him, "all over your jeans."

"What sort of things did Philip Lloyd tell you?"

For a moment she hesitated. "They were secrets."

"Go on."

Chapter Six

They were held back by the slow crawl of traffic leaving the city in the evening, and so the sky was already almost dark when the coach drew up in front of school and the passengers spilled out, stiff-kneed.

"I thought we'd never get here—like a funeral procession it was!"

"It could be chips tonight!"

"I say, did you notice Dan Agnew and Annette!"

"We'll need to watch that!"

"Dan never talked to a girl in his life before!"

"All the way back he was at it!"

"Her eyelids were fluttering, I could feel the draught from where I was sitting!"

"Couldn't hear a word, though—could you?"

"Not a word."

It was agreeable to have something small and domestic to chew over after the solemnity of the Art Gallery, something funny, and on their own scale.

Once disembarked everyone streaked for home without delay, in case Mr Bingham intended to make another speech. Tea and a magazine or a goggle at the box were the things they needed and they set about seeking them.

Dan was glad to be on his own, and that Annette hadn't any funny ideas about walking down the hill with him. He wanted peace to get his thoughts sorted into some kind of order inside his spinning and rejoicing head. What happened next? With success at his fingertips he mustn't make a mess of things now. This was the way he felt—this dizzy triumph—when he knew for a certainty that the ball at his foot was destined for the net, when he understood how to do the problem but hadn't yet got it down on paper; when after a long run of bad luck things started to come right at last.

The night sky was bright with stars. The donkeys in Big Joe's field, surprised by the procession of school-children trundling down the road at this unexpected hour, came to the gate, pushing and curious. The wood of the gate gleamed as if frost was about and the breath of the animals shone whitely. This was the kind of weather that would be welcome on Bonfire Night in four days' time. The pyramid for the bonfire had been built to a tolerable height in the school yard already, and during the past week most children arriving at school had added branches, broken boxes, bundles of old newspaper and rags to it. The Art Class were known to have a fabulous guy on the production line. After next week the fireworks would be taken out of the shop windows to make more room for Christmas cards. Already there was a little Christmas tree standing in the window of Eventide Home. The Oldies believed in making their Christmas go a very long way.

Dan turned the corner and had walked slap into the square of light on the ground. This time he had forgotten to remind himself that he mustn't expect it, and there it was! It pulled him to a halt, and he stood staring down at his own ankles as if they had become entangled in a patch of luminous barbed wire. He looked up and saw the light shining from the window of his father's shop.

Careful. Easy. Don't get fooled the same way twice. You thought it was Dad in the workshop and it was Mum—remember? Probably it's Mum in there now; she's come back to find out if any of the spiders who got away have dared to show up again. Of course it's Mum. Don't expect it to be anyone else. And then he heard the whine of the electric saw and knew that this time it was his father who was in the workshop.

Dan didn't move at once. He stood pulling great gulps of cold air deep into his lungs and letting them go again until he felt steady, because he knew that what happened next would be difficult and very important. It had to happen some time. Because of what he had learned from Annette it was going to happen now. At last he stepped out of the light on the ground and crossed the darkness to the workshop door.

"Dad?" His father had his back to him. Dan had to speak loud because the motor of the saw was still running.

"Hallo there, son."

"Busy?"

"That's right."

This is what we always say. These are the words, we

have used them thirty times or more every term since I was old enough to come back from school on my own. I can't remember what we say next. Once I begin to think about what I am going to say nothing that I say will sound true and easy. The words spin and get muddled or else they come out stiff and pompous, not like Dad and me talking. I could ask him what he's working at. I can't see from where I am. But that isn't what I've come for.

"Dad. There's something I want to say."

Dad must have known from his voice that it was something special because he put his hand to the switch of the saw and turned it off. If Dad was thinking with his hands he needed to stop work before he could do any other thinking. Silence was stretched out between them.

"Well, what is it?"

The only way to begin was to say it. "I want to talk about what happened to Philip Lloyd."

He saw Dad's shoulders stiffen but still he didn't turn round. "What is it you want to say?"

"I don't think it was your fault that his bike went into the wall."

"I see. You wanted to tell me that."

This was the way you talked to a child, as if you were playing a game, getting down on your hands and knees. "Come on—let's pretend."

"I don't think there was anything wrong with Philip's brakes," Dan said.

"A great many people in the town wouldn't agree with you."

"I've found out something, Dad. I think I know what happened that day, what Philip was doing."

"He was going down the hill too fast for safety. That was what," Dad said.

"He was going down the hill without using any brakes. He'd been dared to," Dan said.

"Silly young fool."

Dan hadn't expected it to be like this. This wasn't the way it ought to happen. If it had been a play on the telly you'd have seen Dad's face close up, crumpling. His eyes would stare and suddenly go wet and his mouth would tighten. He'd turn and cross the workshop floor and take Dan by the shoulders and rock him backwards and forwards a little, saying, "Son! Son!" and they'd go and stand for a long time at the workshop door, looking out at the stars in the sky, before the music came on and the play was over. All that would have been unreal in an embarrassing kind of way, something to think about afterwards and to put up with at the time because of the difference it was going to make to Dad. Maybe Dad didn't understand just what that difference was.

"There's a gang of kids in the school, they go in for that sort of thing."

"I daresay. Children are like that."

Couldn't he be more interested? Didn't he see how much it mattered? Dan decided to play his top card.

"It's Roger, Dad. He's made himself the big boss. He bullies the kids and puts them up to all kinds of crazy things. They're afraid of him."

Dan waited for Dad to hit the roof. Things had

93

happened so neatly, he couldn't have done it better if he'd been able to arrange them himself. Now Dad was put in the clear and Roger condemned to everlasting disgrace.

Dad said, "Roger's father used to be a bit of a bully, as I remember. I daresay Roger gets a taste of it."

"Was Uncle Bill really like that?" Go on. Tell me.

For a long time his father didn't speak. At last he said "It would be a pity if your uncle and aunt were to get word of what you've told me."

That wasn't what Dad had said, it couldn't have been.

"When this gets around," Dan said explosively, "everyone will know!"

"If it gets around." His father was setting some tools on the bench as if it mattered very much that each tool was lying straight and evenly spaced from the next one.

"You mean you aren't going to tell them?"

"No."

"But Dad——!" He knew he was red-faced and stammering like a kid. At last his father turned but now Dan didn't want to look at him.

"Listen to me, Dan."

"All right. I can hear." He put all the rudeness he could into the words. Come on, let's have your excuses, anything for a quiet life, that's always the way it is with you. I don't need to see the expression on your face, I know that apologetic look that means you're backing out of whatever unpleasant or difficult thing it is that has to be done. But why does it hurt so much, seeing the things that are wrong in the people who matter? It is unfair.

"Your Uncle Bill is my brother, remember."

"So what?"

"It would finish Roger at the school if this got out."

"I daresay."

"Think of it. What would it be like at Christmas when we go to spend the day with your uncle and aunt?"

Why bring Christmas into it? That isn't fair either. Christmas is different. Christmas is neutral and ought to be kept out of a mess like this. Once a year, because it's Christmas, I'm really fond of Aunt Florence and Uncle Bill. I don't expect to be but I am, even when she does her Lady Bountiful act, even Uncle Bill and his heartiness and his cigar.

Dad said, "Anyway, we can't be absolutely sure that it happened the way you say it did."

"Almost sure. That was one of the crazy things they used to challenge each other to do—the long hill with no brakes. It was on their list, I know that much. They took it in turns to choose something off the list and do it. Roger made them. Philip was scared stiff of Roger, I know that too."

"Did Philip tell anybody he was going to do this?"

"No. He'd have told them afterwards."

"Have you thought it's possible I did make a mistake when I was adjusting the brakes on Philip's bike?"

Dan's scorn was loud and immediate. "A mistake! You! You know you never made that sort of mistake in your life!" He was glad he succeeded in making it sound like an insult. That was the way it was intended.

"Everyone can make mistakes. We all have to accept that."

Dan was glad to feel his hot anger streak suddenly right through him and take charge. "Talk about accepting it! You! You never accepted it, did you? It was because people blamed you for the accident that you stopped coming into the shop, not because of what happened to Philip. It was because of that that you shut yourself away. Oh, you were sorry about Philip all right, but what about being sorry for Mum and me for a change? What do you suppose all this has been like for us?"

He stopped being angry as soon as he had spoken. Moment stretched into moment, the continued silence chained them together. At last his father said, "I'm sorry. Yes, I'm sorry, Dan."

That's what I should be saying, we've got the parts mixed up, it's always me who has to be sorry to Dad. What do I say if he tells me he is sorry?

Dad was asking, "Can Roger be prevented from doing what you say he is doing?"

"Yes."

"Can you be sure of that?"

"Quite sure. I'll keep my eyes skinned."

"Who knows about this as well as you?"

"Nobody, not for sure."

"It mustn't happen again. I'd speak to Roger myself, of course, only probably the fewer people who are involved the better." Probably Dad meant what he said, but it sounded lame, and prompted Dan to declare, "There isn't any need for you to do a thing. We'll

96

hammer him." He had no idea how or by whom the hammering would be done but he had a vision of a just cause and an army of avenging heroes who would come when he beckoned. His father's tameness made him more confident of his own power.

"You don't prove anything by fighting, Dan."

How do you prove things, then? Come on, tell me. Fighting is the only way, whether it's the telly or an argument after school. The Big Boys win every time.

"You prove you're bigger," Dan said.

"So long as that's all you want to prove."

Dan didn't understand, didn't want to. Probably when they were kids Uncle Bill used to kick Dad around and Dad had worked out this way of thinking for his own comfort. Perhaps Roger was lucky to have a father who shouted and threw things. Then you could shout back. But it took two to make a success of shouting.

Dad was speaking again. "Actually, Dan, I've been making a start here myself today."

"You've what?" He'd heard the first time, but let him say it again.

"See here. Ash. I cut them the other morning, up in the woods. I was trimming them when you came in. Just the job, don't you think?" He was holding a staff cut from an ash tree in his hand, other staves were propped against the bench, seven of them, eight altogether.

"Still have to steam them and bend them over—that's the tricky part of the operation. About four feet in length Mr Bingham said, didn't he? You can tell him I'll have them for him in two or three days."

So Mr Bingham's shepherds would have their crooks, after all. Joe and Co. would be armed against bears, wolves and robbers, Dan would have no more need to think up apologies for his father, Roger would have to find a new reason for a smile on his face. If this had happened yesterday Dan would have let out a great whoop of delight, a whole load of worry would have slipped off him, it would have been like scooping the jack-pot on the fruit machine. And his father was standing there balancing an ash branch across his palm smiling an unsure half-smile, waiting for Dan to be pleased and grateful and astonished. But there was nothing that he could say. If he'd been talking to some-one else he could have turned his mouth up at the corners and purred, "How super! How terrific!" as he'd taught himself to do when one of Mum's smiling colourless cousins gave him a hopeless kind of a book for his birthday, or his fifth biro, or a tie that he wouldn't have dressed up a cat in. But he couldn't put on that sort of act with Dad. This was another thing that was unfair.

Dad had the sense to see that he was struck dumb, and told him he'd better clear off home. "Your mother will be looking out for you. I've a little more work to do here before I come. Tell her that." Muddled and angry, ashamed and unsatisfied, Dan let himself out of the workshop and closed the door behind him. Even the sweep of the lighthouse, punctual as ever, soft as milk across his face, did nothing to ease him tonight.

So at the next rehearsal, on the evening before Bonfire Night, the shepherds were furnished with a crook apiece. Everyone said how splendid they were, Mr Bingham was most enthusiastic. "I knew your father would make a splendid job of them, Dan."

They were rehearsing in costume, not full regalia, but basic draperies, white garments for angels, dressing-gowns for Kings, bedspreads for shepherds. "Enough to give us the flavour of it," Mr Bingham said, "to let us feel the atmosphere. Everyone ready and in their places? Action!"

They tried. Indeed they tried. Everyone knew his words—and everyone else's words—backwards by now, they all understood exactly what they had to do and when and how they had to do it. Perhaps that was the trouble. When the same words are repeated time after time in the same kind of voice they stop meaning what they say, and going through the same movements over and over again doesn't make them look any easier or more natural. They were puppets, they were clock-work toys, there was no surprise left in anything that they did or said.

"Action!" They fidgeted and itched their way through the words and the movements again, two of the shepherds got their staves entangled and Mr Bingham sighed and said other words down his nose that they wished they could have heard. It was obvious that Mary knew what the Angel Gabriel had to tell her before he said it. The Good Tidings of Great Joy had been in yesterday's newspaper.

They wished it was this time tomorrow night. There

would be no rehearsal tomorrow. The bonfire, big and black as a mountain, was waiting out there in the school yard. It had grown another foot or two in height since yesterday. It was taller than last year's bonfire had been. Tomorrow it would be a blaze of spurting, leaping flames. Smoke from it would wind like ropes into the sky, there would be rockets carving their path upwards and exploding in joyful coloured rain, and Catherine wheels and unexpected squibs. The girls would squeal and jump about. But most of all there would be the bonfire.

"Take that scene again. Everybody ready?" Mr Bingham said. It was impossible, it was almost indecent that any man could remain so patient. "Take it through again. You and your companions are watching your sheep on the hills above Bethlehem and suddenly——!" Mr Bingham waved his hand towards the window where the evening sky had turned deep blue, the colour of ink. "Action!"

"There's someone out there," Joe said.

Everyone sat up and took notice. That wasn't what Joe was meant to say, those words weren't in the script. Joe was staring out of the window. "There is someone. Over there. I'm sure."

"Come along," Mr Bingham chided, "let's not waste any more time——"

"It isn't just one person, it's lots of them. I think they're—yes, over there by the bonfire! They're messing about over at our bonfire! Come on!"

If it was action Mr Bingham was after he'd got it.

They left their appointed stations, angels, shepherds, Kings, attendants, and crowded at the window. "Now then!" Mr Bingham protested but no one paid any heed. They could see what Joe had seen, figures moving darkly round the bonfire, a flicker of a match, a drift of smoke. The flicker of the match had shown them something else, pale hands but no faces. The faces were hidden by masks. This gave them their clue, they knew who the trespassers were.

"The Wreckers! It's them!"

"Come to burn up our bonfire!"

"I'd like to see them try!"

"That's who it is—the Wreckers!"

They wrenched at the window and flung it wide. Over the sill they poured, hitching up their long garments to their knees to make the crossing easier. They streamed out across the school yard.

"Our bonfire!"

"Come on!"

No one needed urging. Joe and his shepherds formed the spearhead of the attack, with Sid among them. The rest of them followed closely, whooping vengeance. It was their first unrehearsed action for weeks and it was magnificent, no one waited to be told what to do or asked for a script. Mr Bingham, following agitatedly in their wake, pitched forward as he went through the window and fell hard on the concrete, but no one noticed or came back to help him to his feet. They stampeded out into the frosty darkness, yelling, ripe for combat.

Joe and Co. armed with their staves were the first to

come within striking distance. The Wreckers saw them advancing and knew they were outnumbered. Some of them fled while they had opportunity, but most stood their ground. A dozen fights were joined, the shepherds' crooks thwacked and prodded and hooked at alien ankles, Sid, Roger and Dan were busy with their feet and their fists; the girls, hampered a little by their draperies, were tiptoe on the edge of the rumpus, ready and eager to seize any opportunity to tweak and trip and pinch.

At last the enemy had had enough of it, they turned and fled over the wall, sent on their way with triumphant jeers and a last punch for the journey.

Breathless and exultant the victors gulped congratulations at each other and felt their bruises.

"We did it!"

"What a nerve! Coming up here!"

"Our bonfire!"

"The bonfire! Quick! The bonfire!"

They had not noticed that the Wreckers' plan to set light to their bonfire had almost succeeded. From an oily rag stuffed into the heap a long sour cord of smoke with a hint of flame in it was creeping.

"It's alight!"

"Get it out! Quick!"

Again the shepherds' crooks came into action. Cunningly hooked into the smouldering pile they pulled out what had been set alight and many willing feet scattered it and trampled it dead. At last there was no more smoke, no whiff of danger. Tomorrow, not tonight, the Headmaster's torch would be thrust into the dry bowels of the bonfire and it would burn for them. Their bonfire was saved.

It was only when the crisis was over that the victors heard the applause and realized they had an audience. They stared at the figures who had halted on the road and were watching them across the wall, and clapping.

"You sent them about their business!"

"You soon taught them a lesson!"

"Up boys and at 'em! Eh? And girls, too! That's the stuff to give the troops!"

It was the Oldies, a dozen or so of them, with little Mr Anstruther linked firmly in the centre of the group. They noticed there was something peculiar about Mr Anstruther. He was standing in one place but prancing a little, wagging his head and singing, "Oh I do like to be beside the seaside!" in small defiant gusts of song.

Miss Sillitoe, who was holding Mr Anstruther as if he were a self-willed bicycle which she was tryng to steer, explained, "Poor Mr Anstruther, he isn't quite himself this afternoon. We thought a little walk in the night air would help him before we all go back to dear Matron."

They knew what that meant. Mr Anstruther had slipped his lead and stayed too long in The Holly Tree, and they were trying to get him sobered up before tea. "Just up to the end of the road and down again," Miss Sillitoe continued, and all her beads and ear-rings jangled in her effort to get Mr Anstruther upright and keep him there. "We didn't expect to meet you tonight," she went on. "Tomorrow's Bonfire Night, isn't it? Or have you been having a fancy dress party?"

They remembered they were dressed up for the play and explained. The Oldies were enchanted.

"A Nativity Play! How perfectly splendid!"

"Just the very thing for Christmas!"

"Oh how lovely!"

They asked who was to take which of the parts, and when the play was to be performed, and the children told them.

"And all your fathers and mothers and brothers and sisters will be coming to see it, will they?"

They nodded glumly. Indeed they would, grannies, second cousins and all.

"Would it seem very forward of us——" Miss Sillitoe hesitated, every bead and inch of ribbon on her quivering. "Do you think perhaps there might be a chance that we——?"

They saw what she was fishing for and said they would ask Mr Bingham. He would be the person to ask. They promised to speak to him about it.

"Oh would you?"

"That really would be something for us to look forward to!"

"A real treat it would be!"

Mr Bingham? But where was Mr Bingham all this time? Where had he been while the fight was going on? Where was he now? Why wasn't he hauling them indoors this minute and distributing the blame like the Wrath of God where he considered blame to be due? It wasn't like Mr. Bingham to fade out on an occasion such as this, he must have heard the rumpus. He should have been blowing his eloquent top.

"Last time I remember seeing him I think he was coming out through the window after us."

"Where has he got to now?"

And they retraced their steps back to the open window of the classroom, to look for Mr Bingham.

Chapter Seven

"After all," Fred reminded them in his pious voice, as if his newly-laundered soul had just come crackling out of its cellophane wrapping, "this is the Season of Goodwill."

"We know, we know," Joe complained, "it isn't goodwill we're short of, it's cash! Bonfire Night about cleaned me out."

"Me too!"

"Still, it was the best year we ever had! Those rockets! Talk about blast off!"

"It couldn't have been a better night for it!"

Today the air was thick as a blanket and grey. It was pouring, the hillside was streaked with streams and they had all had to spend their break in the classroom.

Fred had taken this chance to corner them. "Come on—fork out!"

"People in hospital don't really want bunches of flowers! I know I wouldn't!" Megan declared.

Joe told her that was why he hadn't sent the roses, the time she had chickenpox.

"I'm sorry for Mr Bingham and all that," Annette

said, "but wouldn't it be all right if we just sent him a card?"

"A card isn't the same."

"It depends who it's from—and we could all sign it. After all, it's the thought that counts," Annette said, hoping that this sentiment, and her eyelids, were having some effect on Dan though it didn't look like it.

"Well, I know what I think," said Sid, "if a person can't step out across a window-sill without falling flat on his face and knocking himself senseless, we don't need to spend our money buying him flowers."

"What with Christmas coming up and all——"

"And no way of earning extra cash at this time of year!"

"It wasn't even as if he'd been wrapped up in a bed-spread like we were."

"If he'd just looked where he was going——"

"I suppose he tripped himself up like that because he was dead keen to barge right in on our fight and stop it."

"You can say that again."

They remembered their joyful victory over the Wreckers, Joe and his lads laying about them, Sid in the thick of it, never wasting a punch. In a way it had been obliging of Mr Bingham to trip coming through that window. Perhaps after all he deserved his bunch of flowers. Someone said fruit might be better.

"Fruit costs the earth at this time of year," Fat Margie warned. She knew. Of course it was only the price of fruit that was preventing her from keeping to the slimming diet in her Mum's magazine. Of course it was.

"Ten pence apiece would just about do it," Fred calculated.

Roger felt about in his pockets and slapped the money down right away. That was what Sir Roger would do. The others hesitated and did sums, delaying a contribution.

"Busting up his head and his ankle at the same time, that was real clever of him."

"And it's a bad break. He won't be able to walk on it for ages."

"His head's the worst. My auntie works at the hospital, she heard someone say it could be weeks."

"How many weeks?"

This was the question that no one had yet asked outright. Three weeks, four weeks—five weeks, perhaps?

"He could still be in hospital at Christmas," Dan calculated, and those of them who had spent a Christmas in hospital told each other how jolly an occasion it could be, so that they need not feel guilty at wishing Mr Bingham a share in those festivities.

"You never saw so many balloons in your life," Pete reported, "the ward was sprouting with balloons."

"The tree reached right up to the ceiling. We all got presents. The surgeon was Father Christmas. He thought he was very funny."

"As much turkey as we could eat——"

"And the nurses came round the wards with lanterns, singing carols."

"They've got some smashing nurses in hospital."

Oh, fortunate Mr Bingham, falling flat on his face through that window!

No one had yet dared to speculate openly what might happen to them while Mr Bingham was enjoying the nurses and the balloons, but at the back of each of their minds there stirred a faint, unexpressed, hardly acknowledged prickle of hope that the performance of the Nativity Play, lacking Mr Bingham's leadership, might be, would have to be, called off. How could they be expected to carry on without Mr Bingham's masterly direction? Of course they couldn't, Mr Bingham *was* the play. Without him in command it would just fall apart, even with him it was already showing the daylight. He might have realized this. Probably in the comfort of his hospital bed he would be glad that the only striped shepherds he would encounter this Christmas would be those on his Christmas cards. Falling through that window was the best thing Mr Bingham could have done. Deliverance all round with honour was made possible. It was almost too good to be true.

Annette reported that Miss Sillitoe and Mr Anstruther had been sighted calling on the Headmaster yesterday.

"I'll bet they were asking him for tickets."

"Bang in the front row!"

"They were madly keen to come."

"It would make their Christmas, they said."

"And Mr Jason Jonson was up seeing the Head this morning, too!"

"Oh—him! Of course he'd want to be there!"

They all knew about Mr Jason Jonson by this time; word of his shameful deception had seeped through from Annette and Margie. All his glamour melted at once, he was a silly old show-off, he had injured them with his airs, they had felt this way when they were kids and found out about Father Christmas. He richly deserved to have his seat in the front row cancelled.

"You fork out ten pence all round and we'll order that basket of fruit," Fred decided, and this time they agreed with him and forked.

They were cruising down the corridor on their way to singing class after break when Sid spotted the new notice on the board.

"Hi! Have you seen this?"

They braked, piling up and pushing.

"That means us."

"Do you suppose——?"

Of course they supposed. Of course the Headmaster wished to see the cast of the Nativity Play in the Library after school so that he could hand them out their discharge.

"We're going to get our cards all right," Dan exulted.

"We must be sorry." Annette was remembering with a small twinge of regret how heavenly she had looked in her halo. "It would be more polite if we were a little sorry."

They agreed to be as sorry as was necessary and careered on to singing class to join in "Then let us be joyful" from the bottoms of all their grateful hearts.

The Headmaster was waiting for them in the Library after school. They were surprised to find Mr Jason Jonson with him. What did he think he was doing? How could he sit there so calmly, stroking his chin and smiling at them? His long elegant legs were crossed so that his apricot silk socks shone like twin sunbeams.

His patterned cravat flaunted itself against his plum corduroy lapels. They hardened their hearts against him and waited to hear what the Headmaster had to say. They noticed that he was wearing his platform manner.

"Sit down, no talking, listen to what I have to tell you, any questions afterwards." They took their places, trying to prepare their faces to look suitably sorry as soon as the good news broke.

"I'm sure you will all be glad to know that I have heard from the hospital that Mr Bingham is making excellent progress from his injuries." They registered modified pleasure while suspicion cooled their hearts. Whoever's aunt it was who had said Mr Bingham would be a long time in hospital had evidently got it wrong.

"His doctors, however, advise him not to return to school until the commencement of the Spring Term."

They took their cue from Annette, who had dropped her mouth open like an apprehensive codfish. This wasn't easy to do because inside their heads joy bells had now begun to ring inconveniently loudly.

"This means, of course, that he cannot continue all the work and organization he has put into the rehearsals of the Nativity Play for the end of term."

Annette blinked and blew her nose. The other Sob Sisters admired her and wished they had thought of doing it first.

"I know how much disappointment it would cause to you and your families and the rest of the school—and indeed to our many friends throughout the town—if the tradition of the Annual Play were to be broken."

What did he mean? "If"? "Were to be"? Swinging between hope and despair they forgot about their faces and yearned for what was coming next. Let him get on with it.

"I was right when I said the school had many friends in the town. One of these friends, hearing of our predicament, has stepped forward generously to offer us his services." Here the Headmaster inclined his nose in the direction of Mr Jason Jonson and smiled. Mr Jason Jonson returned the smile to the Headmaster.

"Mr Jason Jonson needs no introduction to anybody in this town. You all know of his high standing in the world of the theatre, and I am sure you will appreciate his kindness in stepping into the breach and offering to take over from Mr Bingham the office of producer of the play."

"A pleasure, Headmaster," Mr Jason Jonson said. "Bad luck on Bingham, but as we say in the Profession 'The play must go on'!"

His voice oozed pleasantness; they toughened their faces, protecting themselves against it. They knew from the Headmaster's expression that this was where they were expected to clap but no one clapped. No one batted an eyelid in case it might sound like applause. They stared blankly at Mr Jason Jonson, who maintained his smile. The Headmaster's eyebrows rose up a good inch into his forehead and stayed there, appealing to them to be impressed and amazed and overjoyed. They refused to be any of these things. He might as well have been talking to them in a foreign language. Probably it was Chinese.

Silence became uncomfortable, like stretched elastic. At last the Headmaster allowed his eyebrows to slide into a frown. "I don't need to tell you what extremely privileged people you are," he said, telling them all the same just in case they hadn't got the message, "nor do I need to state what high hopes we will all entertain this year of a really notable performance."

He smiled at them threateningly and gathered up his papers. "Over to you," he said to Mr Jason Jonson, and left the room.

Mr Jason Jonson uncoiled his long legs and stood up, confronting them. It was surprising that he could stand upright in the full force of their disappointment and rage and mistrust. Any lesser man would have toppled, withered up, evaporated. But there he was, still able to smile, still attempting to gather them in with his glance, the way an actor does when he comes to the front of the stage to acknowledge the applause, humble and proud at the same time.

He spread his hands in their direction. "Well, whether we like it or not, chaps, that's the way it is," he said. "I've worked in a great many roles in a great many theatres, as you know, but a Nativity Play is a new field for me, and I accept it as a challenge."

Their eyes might have told him that he was right about the challenge, but he was still viewing them kindly across the glow of imaginary footlights, kidding himself that he was talking to friends.

"We shall learn a great deal about each other while

we are engaged on this exercise," he said, "and I must say that I for one am looking forward to it."

It was this statement that brought Fat Margie to her feet. She stood up, and before she had opened her mouth the rest of them knew what she was going to say and were solid behind her, every one of them. There were times when it was necessary to be honest, and Margie, in whose life honesty played such an inconvenient and necessary part, was the right person to say what must now be said.

"Mr Jason Jonson please——"

"Yes, my dear?"

"There is something I want to say."

"Splendid! Splendid! Say on!" He sat down comfortably, ready to be told how privileged and unworthy they felt to be working under his direction.

They waited for Margie to make a start, wondering what words she would choose. There was something fine and heroic about Fat Margie standing there twisting her hands and swallowing, hunting for words in which to say what was impossible.

"What part are you taking in the play, child?" Mr Jason Jonson asked to make it easier for her to begin.

She mumbled that she was an angel and then jumped in off the deep end.

"Mr Jason Jonson, when we were at the Art Gallery looking at Christmas pictures this term with Mr Bingham we went into the Reference Library, and there was a book there called *The Actors' and Entertainers' Who's Who*."

She had got so far. Mr Jason Jonson already knew

114

where she was heading. They could tell as much by his expression. All at once his face appeared to change gear; you learn how to do that when you are an actor. He was getting himself ready for a disappointment. They realized that during his career he must have had plenty of practice. Their eyes slid away from him, they didn't want to watch him any longer. They stared at their own tightened knuckles and waited for Margie to go on.

"In this book there are lists of actors and actresses, anyone who has been at all important, and it tells all about them and the parts they played. The man at the Library asked if we wanted to look up anybody special, and one of us looked up your name, Mr Jason Jonson, and it wasn't there. There wasn't anything about you."

Fat Margie sat down abruptly. She had done briefly and with dignity what was necessary. They hoped she wasn't going to cry now and spoil it. Her cheeks grew fuller and more pink and her chin was uncertain.

Mr Jason Jonson was on his feet again and they were compelled to look at him. From her place beside Margie Annette volunteered that the man in the Library had said there might have been a mistake. Names were left out of the book sometimes, he said.

"No, there wasn't any mistake. You needn't have looked for my name in that volume, it isn't there." He was staring out of the window as if he recognized their scalding embarrassment and was anxious to let them off as lightly as he could. "I was never sufficiently—important"—he used Margie's word deliberately—"to qualify for an entry in *The Actors' and Entertainers' Who's Who*."

"But—Mr Jason Jonson!" They leapt unanimously to defend him. "Everyone knows! You've often told us yourself!"

"I'm afraid I have allowed you to be too generous in your rating of me," he said, "too generous by far. The world of the theatre is a much vaster one than any of you can imagine, and few people get to the top of the tree. I have, it is true, played a great many roles in a great many plays, but the big parts always"—he put out his hands and they could see the opportunities slipping through his fingers like fish—"they always eluded me. And my love for my work has made me appear more illustrious than my performances warranted—you know how it is."

Yes, they knew. His honesty wounded them but they were full of gratitude to him for being able to be honest and elegant at the same time. Not many men could have done it.

Mr Jason Jonson pushed the knot of his cravat a little tighter against his long neck and said, "So now you can tell me something."

They were ready by this time to tell him anything. He only had to ask, they'd tell him. Anything.

"This Nativity Play of yours—how do you think it's coming along?"

There was no need for Annette or anyone else to provide them with a cue. "It isn't!" they exploded. Oh the relief of being able to say this out loud to somebody who wanted to know, who would listen and believe them. "It's terrible. And we're wrong, all of us."

Mr Jason Jonson stroked his nose and smiled at them "You are, are you?"

"Nothing we do is right," they told him, "we try, we try, honest."

"None of us can do more than that," he said. "So now let's get along to see Miss Hunt and tell her our news, we might look at the props and run through a few of the scenes." And when he stalked out of the Library they fell in behind him, united as an army.

He didn't seem as impressed as they had hoped he might be by the abundance of haloes and wings, the wealth of turbans, crowns, caskets, mantles and bed-spreads. His fingers flicked through them. "Properties are always the least important, it's the play and the people who matter."

Miss Hunt, hovering and twittering in the fore-ground, had obviously expected more enthusiasm. She explained the significance of each detail, how carefully it had been executed, and how strongly Mr Bingham had approved of her handiwork. "A touch of the bizarre about the three Kings, we thought, just a touch. The cloak for Joseph, we've kept it as unobtrusive as possible, of course. The largest of the haloes is for the Angel Gabriel."

"The shepherds' crooks are good," Mr Jason Jonson commented. He took one of the crooks in his hand, testing its strength and quality. He seemed to know how to handle a crook, what to expect from it and what its uses would be.

His eye had reached the cardboard box which held the doll. His forefinger explored the wrappings of tissue paper and uncovered the doll's face. His own face stiffened.

"And this——?"

They were struck dumb, unable to tell him that this was The Child. Obviously it was Fat Margie's doll, her grandmother had given it to her on her seventh birthday, she called it Amanda Jane.

Mr Jason Jonson spread the tissue paper across the doll's face again. "It won't do, you know," he decided. They knew it wouldn't do. Even Miss Hunt raised no protest.

He inquired who was playing Mary and Megan was propelled to the front. "Oh, it's you, is it? Well, what do you want an—object like this for when you've got a perfectly good baby at home?"

Megan looked at him blackly and growled that she couldn't bring the Kid, if that was what he meant. He would yell. He would be certain sure to yell. "He yells quite a bit, and when he sees a crowd of people he doesn't recognize dressed up in funny clothes——"

Mr Jason Jonson interrupted her. "What makes you think there wasn't any crying in the stable that night? You bring that child along with you to the next rehearsal."

It was a command. Megan gulped rebelliously and tried to melt into the background. "You come right here in the middle," he told her and asked who played Joseph.

Fred had been waiting for this. It gave him great pleasure to present himself.

"He stands at the back," Annette explained, but

Mr Jason Jonson told Fred to come and stand beside Mary, and then he identified and lined up the other characters till he knew what part everyone was taking.

"Glad to meet you," he said. "Now let's take it through. And remember—none of it is easy."

It wasn't easy, no easier than it had been at any of the previous rehearsals, but it was different. In the first scene the Angel Gabriel was allowed to say his piece without interruption.

"Terrified, weren't you?" Mr Jason Jonson asked Megan when Pete had finished, and Megan agreed that she was.

"That's right," he said, and told Pete to take it through again. "Remember an angel is a voice not a person," and Pete knew what he meant and became a voice.

Now the shepherds were in the fields keeping watch over their flocks by night. Joe's chilblains were wild today. Every winter Joe had chilblains. For a week they had been raging like animals, he couldn't keep his feet or his hands still.

Mr Jason Jonson saw him scratching and stamping. "It's the frost that does it," he said, "it can be bitter cold up there on those hills at night," and the shepherds pulled the thick folds of their cloaks closer to protect their faces against that icy upland air.

Now the sky had become crowded and bright with angels, so bright that the shepherds could not bear to look at them. "Your own shadows on the ground, that's what you're looking at, isn't it?" Mr Jason Jonson asked, and of course he was right, their own shadows thrown by the brilliance of the angels.

"Take it once more," Mr Jason Jonson said when the angels had gone away again into heaven, "and remember you are delivering the happiest news that the world has had since its creation," and he smiled and the angels smiled all together.

Now the Holy Family were in the stable, and when the shepherds had visited them it was time for the three Kings to come. Today there were four Kings. Mr Jason Jonson had joined the procession, Caspar, Baltazar and Melchior followed him. Whatever treasure it was that Mr Jason Jonson's empty hands were carrying so carefully it must certainly have been singular and exquisite.

"When we set off from our kingdoms we didn't think we would finish our journey kneeling on the floor of a stable, did we?" he said, and knelt. This was how a king knelt. None of his pomp and circumstance mattered, neither did any of the things he had done or the things he had not been able to do. All his life he had been on his way to this stable.

Mr Jason Jonson got up off the stable floor, dusting the knees of his trousers. "Rehearsal with choir and recorders tomorrow after school, and on the next day. And now get off home."

It was dark outside. The air was cold. White mist clung in ragged patches along the hillside. The puddles in the school yard were lightly frozen over and crackled when they tramped across them. Out at sea the lighthouse was at work. The street lamps shone like beads along the sea front. A jewelled caterpillar of a train crept out of the tunnel, bound for the station.

"The five forty-two, we're late," Dan said, slipping back into the comfortable company of the things he knew and understood. He was walking home with Sid and hoped Sid wouldn't want to talk.

"It was different today, wasn't it?" Sid volunteered, and Dan agreed, "You can say that again." He wondered what Roger had thought of it. Roger's opinion might have been interesting.

"Roger," he asked Sid, "is he still around?"

"No. He cleared off early, with some kids."

"He—what?"

"Those kids who run his errands for him, the ones he plays the big boss with, you know."

All the arguments and debates that Dan had been chewing over and had pushed unresolved into the back of his mind crowded forward.

"He's gone off with those kids—are you sure?"

"I told you."

"Which way?"

"How would I know?"

"Come on!"

Sid stared. "What do you mean? Come on where?"

Dan broke into a run.

Chapter Eight

It wasn't true that Dan had forgotten about Roger altogether, but after he had broken the tremendous news of his villainy to Dad and been so bitterly disappointed by Dad's reaction, other affairs became more important and he was glad to fill his mind with them. The magnificent fight with the Wreckers, Mr Bingham's timely accident, the roar and glory of Bonfire Night, speculation about the future of the Nativity Play—there was plenty to push Roger and Ronnie Simpson and the other squealing kids into the background. "We'll hammer him!" he had boasted to his father, hoping that some of the scorn he felt for Dad's mildness was showing through. Oh, he'd been very confident about the justice he intended to deliver. What was Dad on about? Fighting was the only thing some people understood. He would see to it that Roger was beaten. Up the avenging heroes!

One day last week, while Mum was out, his father had asked, "That business with Roger—did you get that fixed up?"

"I told you. It'll be taken care of."

"Are you sure? It mustn't happen again. Unless you're sure, Dan, I ought to have a word with Roger myself—"

Although he was acting more like his old self and would speak to Roger if he had to, Dad's reluctance to do so was evident. Dan felt larger and more scornful than ever. He assured his father that everything would be all right.

"If you're sure—" Did Dad have to look so relieved?

With a jerk of conscience Dan realized that that was a week ago and he hadn't done a thing. And now Roger was off with that gaggle of kids again, and one wretched kid among them at this moment might be choosing between two terrors, while Roger supervised his choice.

He broke into a trot as soon as they reached the road. "Come on, we've got to hurry!"

Sid at his elbow protested, "Look, what is all this?"

"Tell you afterwards—come on!"

His feet stumbled and slid where the road's surface was polished and treacherous with frost. His schoolbag bumped at his back and his breath hurt. Already he had difficulty in keeping up with Sid, who moved, as he always did, with the ease of a well-tuned piece of machinery. They had reached and passed the gate of the donkeys' field long before the animals' curiosity had brought them to it. But it was reassuring to have Sid beside him, he would be a useful partner when the fighting started. Sid would have to be told.

Sid didn't need to be told. Without slacking pace he

asked, "Roger's been bossing those kids around too much, has he?"

"Something like that."

Now they were at the bottom of the hill, where the road from school joined the sea-front. In neither direction was there any sign of Roger and the kids.

"Which way have they gone?"

"We'll try this way first!"

Most people were home by now, the pavements were deserted and the blinds had been pulled down in front of many of the shops. They slowed their pace for a moment at each of the dark entries between the blocks of buildings, but always drew a blank. They climbed the railing of the Scout Hall to examine the bicycle shed but found no one. They skirted the car park. A few figures were loitering around the Fish Saloon which would soon be opening, but there was no sign of Roger and his companions. They dodged through the amusement arcade. This was dark, the machines were unlit and locked and no one was about. Now they had come to the end of the shops. They scanned the area of the boating lake, but except for the family of concrete gnomes it was uninhabited. They examined the edges of the putting green where the low sprawling bushes would afford some cover for private assembly.

"They aren't here!"

"Come on!"

They searched all four sides of each of the beach shelters as they reached them, but they were empty. The tide was high and every small collapsing wave measured out for them the time that was already lost.

"We've got to find them."

"Where else can they have gone?"

"Try the changing rooms."

Sid hoisted himself expertly over the wall of the outdoor bathing pool, and after a moment or two reappeared to report that he had found no one there.

"Maybe I was wrong. Maybe Roger isn't with the kids. They could all be safe home by now."

Better find out. Ronnie Simpson's Dad was a tobacconist. The family lived over the shop, the last of the row of shops. Dan and Sid doubled back. The shop was still open, the bell on the door rang as they pushed it, and they wondered what excuse they could invent if Ronnie was there. But Mrs Simpson came to the counter, carrying Ronnie's baby sister. No, she smiled, Ronnie wasn't home yet. It was these rehearsals for the play, keeping him ever so late. "I do like a Christmas Play! We'll all be there!" She told the baby to say bye bye, and made her wave a fat stiff hand towards the boys.

Dan went into a telephone box and dialled Roger's number. Aunt Florence's voice answered. "Yes?"

"Is Roger there, please?"

"No, he hasn't come in from school yet. Goodness knows when he'll turn up, it's these rehearsals. Can I give him a message? I'm just going out myself, and his father isn't home yet, but I could leave a note. That is Dan, isn't it?"

He put back the receiver without telling her who it was, imagining how Aunt Florence would shrug and smile at herself in the mirror above the telephone before she put on her coat, pleased because Roger had so many friends.

"Look, this is hopeless," Sid said, "we'll never find them."

"We've got to find them."

It was Sid, pressing ahead again, who finally found them.

"Hi! They're here!"

Beyond the farthest of the beach shelters the promenade dwindled down to a narrow stony cove where visitors rarely came. There was seldom anything to bring them here. Occasionally in the summer a travelling preacher used this place to preach the word to the faithful few. Its harshness and isolation suited him. The distant sounds of the holiday world, the rhythm of the band on the pier, the ice-cream van's singsong, the chatter of far-off transistors, all these helped to emphasize the severity of his message. A few tattered posters from last summer still survived, pasted on boulders. "The End is at Hand", "Prepare to Meet thy God", "Justice is Mine".

Dan and Sid crouched at the wall, looking down into the cover. Yes, Roger was there, occupying the ledge which the preacher used as his pulpit. His back was towards the road. The beam of the lighthouse showed a cluster of kids squatted on the shingle in front of him, like a row of frogs.

"Careful, the kids will see us."

"Shut up and listen; they're not seeing anything except him."

This was true. Their faces were closed to everything

except Roger. Gulls screamed and spun from the cliffs above their heads, the high water sucked the strands of seaweed each time a wave ran up the cove, lifted the small stones at the water's edge and rattled them and let them drop, but the boys didn't hear any of these things. They were cold, they must have been cold in that starved night air, but they didn't know that they were cold.

"Ronnie Simpson, he's there," Dan whispered.

"Like a rabbit."

"They're all like rabbits." Squatting like frogs, scared as rabbits.

"Shut up. Roger's going to talk."

Roger said, "They'll all be sitting comfortably back home with their feet up, won't they?" His audience nodded, an eager row of mandarin dolls. Roger laughed and said, "God bless the box," and they laughed back at him. "That's all they've got, isn't it—the boring old box?"

They nodded, chanting, "The boring old box."

"But we've got something better than that, haven't we?"

"Yes, Roger, yes."

"What have we got that they haven't?"

They knew their responses. "Kicks and risks, thrills and danger!"

"That's right. And if there's any pushing around to be done who does it?"

"We do, Roger!"

"Listen to them," Dan whispered and Sid between his teeth said shut up, he was listening.

Roger singled out Ronnie Simpson. "Glad you've turned up tonight, Ronnie, because if you hadn't we'd have had to come and fetch you. You didn't fancy it the time you had to pay up for not signing on with the gang the night they smashed those ornamental vases outside Eventide, did you?"

"No, Roger."

He turned to the others. "You lot finished off those vases good and proper, didn't you? Nice work!" and they tittered softly, remembering with relish the crash when the heavy stone urns toppled and shattered, and their own power in toppling them.

"People thought it was the Wreckers who'd done it," someone said.

"That suited you all right, didn't it?"

"And they thought it was the Wreckers who put the paint on the seats in the park!"

"Now dry up and listen while I tell you what the adventure for this week is," Roger bade them, and their amusement withered at once. "It's the lamp at the corner opposite the Police Station, the big one. Well —how's that? I thought you'd like it. Come along— who's volunteering?"

They sucked in the sides of their cheeks but no one spoke. Their fear was frozen on their faces. "With a target that size you could hardly miss!" Roger teased. "Come on, someone! Who's going to be this week's hero?"

Another wave ran up the cove and broke. Sid dug an elbow into Dan's ribs and murmured that he wanted to be sick.

"You can't," Dan said.

Two more waves. Then someone piped up, "But Roger, there's always a policeman on duty just inside the door. We wouldn't have a chance!"

"You've got your homes to run back to," Roger told them. "The kids in Vietnam and Bangladesh and Belfast aren't all as lucky. But you're scared, aren't you?"

They accepted this without protest. Of course they were scared. At the beginning it had been exciting to be scared, flattering to be one of the chosen few whom Roger considered to be worth scaring. They shuffled their feet, their fingers played with the stones on the floor of the cove, they huddled closer to each other, remembering now that they were cold. They could have been home by this time, home and bored, warm and ordinary and safe. They knew they were a long way from home.

"The police would be interested if they heard who it really was who'd done those stone urns and put paint on the seats in the park," Roger suggested.

"They couldn't find out, not now!"

"Unless someone told them."

"No one would tell them," they declared and waited for him to agree with them but he didn't speak.

"You—you wouldn't!" they breathed at him.

"Not a word, provided that lamp outside the Police Station gets the treatment before the end of the week."

Sid's warm angry breath filled Dan's ear. "Time we moved in on this, don't you think?"

Dan grabbed his sleeve and held it. "Hang on a minute."

"What for?"

"Just hang on."

One of the small boys mumbled, "Please, Roger, Ronnie Simpson wants to say something."

"Does he now? Well come on then, Ronnie, what are you waiting for?"

Ronnie Simpson, prodded by the boys on either side of him, said miserably, "They say it was you, Roger, who made them smash those vases."

"Me? Did I? I think it was their own bright idea."

"You know it wasn't." Dan hoped the kid was sufficiently angry to prevent himself from crying. It would be a near thing.

Roger said, "You could try telling the police I put you up to it, see if they believe you."

The kids were shifting about uneasily in their places, though their eyes hadn't moved from Roger's face. None of them was enjoying himself now. The magic, if there had been any magic, had gone sour. They ached for home. They blew on their numbed fingers and rubbed stones between their palms to try to restore some feeling to them. They were tired, tired of being afraid, tired of paying for one adventure with another, tired of pretending, tired of lies and half-lies, tired of being terrified heroes. Roger was still smiling at them. It was too dark to see his face distinctly but they knew by his voice that he was smiling.

"No volunteers for the lamp outside the Police Station? Then I'll have to pick someone. Let's see. You

—yes, you, Ronnie Simpson, you're the lucky fellow. You missed the last party, you can have your turn now!"

Ronnie's voice was half squeal, half moan. "Not me! Please not me, Roger! Please not me!"

"And you'll need two assistants on the job." Roger considered which of them he would choose. He was still smiling.

They would stop that smile. There was one way of doing it. The thought stung them alive and the heat came back into their fingers.

No one could be sure who threw the first stone. Perhaps it was Ronnie. But once it had been thrown other stones followed it thick and fast, raining down on Roger, who taken by surprise stood there, trying with his arms and hands to protect his face. Some of the stones hit him, some missed and rattled against the rocks, multiplying themselves with their own echoes. Roger was trying to retreat now, backing down from the projecting platform of rock, but the children had risen and were closing in on him in a half circle, while the stones still flew and fell.

"This is where we come in," Sid smiled at Dan and they eased themselves over the wall and headed down into the confusion.

They were only just in time. The attackers had almost closed on Roger before Sid reached him. Roger had taken one arm from his face and had grabbed the sleeve of the nearest boy, pulling so that the boy fell headlong forward on to the stones and lay there, crying out loud.

131

The barrage of stones slackened momentarily but soon thickened again. The stones were larger now, more accurately aimed. "Come on, who's next?" Roger asked, ducking and dodging.

Dan said, "We are," and Sid and he stepped between Roger and his assailants, barging, slapping and pushing the smaller boys until they retreated and stood a few yards off, their shoulders heaving, their breath loud and painful. Roger had sagged back against the rock face and was holding his cheek which was bleeding.

"Now empty your hands," Dan ordered the kids. "Get a move on, all of you. Get rid of those stones."

The children glared at him, he thought they weren't going to obey. "You heard," Sid warned. One pair of hands was emptied, other stones followed.

"That the lot? Let's see!"

They raised their empty hands for his inspection.

"All right," Dan told them, "clear off now. What are you waiting for?"

Their gaping faces showed they hadn't expected this. But they were glad to go. The cove was full of the tramp of their feet as they skidded and slithered their way up over the stones to the short wiry grass and finally to the safety of the road.

None of the three who were left spoke until the last glad rattle of liberated footsteps had faded. They didn't look like a party of victors. Roger was squatting on the rock, fighting for breath and nursing his face. Dan emptied small stones out of one of his shoes. Sid, panting, wrung water from the edges of his jeans. He had stepped in a rock pool on his way to the rescue. The beam of the lighthouse discovered them briefly.

"We Three Kings!" Sid declaimed and Roger looked up and snapped, "Well, you know what got you the part, don't you?"

Dan snarled, "Shut up, you two, can't you?" and felt sick. Briefly from the railway line he heard the rhythm of a homecoming train, "The six ten" he noted to himself, but there was no comfort in it.

Roger still dabbing blood said, "Well, thanks, any-way, if you hadn't turned up they'd have got me."

Dan told him, "That was what we came out here to do ourselves. We'd found out what you were up to with the kids."

Roger stared. "Go on, then, why don't you?"

"No thanks." He wasn't being noble or kind or any thing like that. There is a moment when it is possible to let all the gathering heat and anger in your brain run down through your body and into your arms and hands, so that hitting becomes possible and necessary. But that moment had passed. Anyway, maybe fighting wasn't the answer.

"I know what you did to Ronnie Simpson," he told Roger. "That evening on the headland. I was watching."

"So what? The silly kid deserved it."

"And you enjoyed it. You worked it so that the rest of them enjoyed it too."

Roger turned his handkerchief to find a clean place and pressed it to his wound. "Listen, Dan—be your age. Those kids have got to have something in their lives, some spice, something. All they've got is Mum and the telly, cotton wool and a life insurance policy."

"They do what you tell them for the good of their health, I suppose." Dan's scorn was icy. "You make me want to throw."

"It doesn't do anybody harm to learn to be afraid," Roger said, "not with the world the way it is."

"Listen to him!" Dan knew by Sid's voice and his tightened stance that he was aching to hit Roger. Once would be enough, just once.

"You keep your hands off me," Roger warned, fielding a trickle of blood that had run down behind his collar.

"What about Philip Lloyd?" Dan asked, and saw Roger stiffen.

"Well, what about him?"

"I want to know about him, what happened."

"I don't know myself, Dan, not for sure. That's the truth."

"You must have some idea. Did he go down that hill without using his brakes because you said he must?"

"No, I never said that. It was one of the things we talked about doing sometimes, we knew it would be crazy, we only talked about it. But if he was idiot enough to try it out——"

"It wouldn't be any of your business, is that what you think?"

"Well—would it?" Dan knew by the smoothness of Roger's voice that he thought he was home, safe and dry.

"Philip could have been killed."

"Please come home now, Roger." Aunt Florence held out her hands to him. "We don't want your Dad to get worked up or anything like that——"

Anything like what? Roger, without speaking, followed his mother to the car. Sid and Dan watched its tail light growing smaller and smaller.

"Better get along home then," Sid said.

Dan wished with all his heart Sid had been angry. But he had seen Sid angry once already this evening; it was too much to hope to see it twice.

Chapter Nine

The day they were waiting for crawled closer. The dress rehearsal was fixed for Saturday morning, and the performance was to be given on Saturday evening. The whole school, even the most junior classes, were coming to the dress rehearsal.

Excitement had been tightening all through the week. Everything waited for the play, nothing that mattered could happen until the play had happened. Even preparations for Christmas were neglected although the first of the Christmas cards were already coming through the letter-boxes with the morning's mail, and the pavement in front of the greengrocer's shop had sprouted a small forest of Christmas trees overnight. Curtains of turkeys with sausage trimmings hung down across the butcher's window.

Rehearsals under Mr Jason Jonson had gone ahead steadily. These rehearsals were different from earlier rehearsals though no one tried to describe how or why. They didn't want to discuss what the difference might mean. After condemning the play so heartily no one was anxious to be the first to show any hope or enthusiasm for it. They wouldn't allow themselves to be kidded, it was still the same play. It might not turn out as terrible as it had threatened to be under Mr Bingham's direction but it would still be pretty terrible. But Mr Jason Jonson undoubtedly knew his stuff and was working hard as if after all his half-failures this was going to be his big success. He was giving it "his all and how", as Joe remarked. He would take care to see they didn't make complete fools of themselves.

By the time the dress rehearsal came along and the scenery had been assembled and they had got their make-up—sorry, their "slap"—on and their wings were at the ready and their crowns in place and their haloes secured and their beards sprouted and their draperies draped and their loins girded, they would get by, and all their fond friends and relations would declare they had been marvellous; of course they wouldn't be marvellous. Anyone who thought they might be on the edge of a miracle swallowed the thought promptly and told no one that the idea of any miracle had for a moment crossed his or her mind.

The Kid was now appearing regularly at rehearsals. His behaviour was unpredictable. Sometimes he howled, sometimes he just whimpered, sometimes he sucked his thumb and hiccuped, occasionally he smiled or slept. Megan let him behave in whatever way he fancied and didn't interfere. Occasionally when he was yelling his loudest she glared at Mr Jason Jonson with a "What did I tell you?" face. After each rehearsal was over she wheeled the pram down the hill at a whirlwind speed.

The photographer from the town's newspaper visited school and took pictures of the principal characters in their costumes. Even the newspaper in the city printed an article about the play. There were notices announcing it in all the shops, everyone was talking about it, everyone was coming—everyone that was, except Dan's Dad. When Dan brought home the pair of tickets that each scholar had been given for his or her parents Mum tucked them behind the clock and said, "You needn't have bothered bringing two, thanks all the same. You know your father never goes out where he'll meet people these days." But Mum was coming, of course. And the Oldies were coming in a body. They had arranged with Matron to have tea an hour earlier than usual on Saturday afternoon, in order that they could all be there. Annette's Mum was closing her Beauty Salon on Saturday, so that she, with two of her chief assistants (a pair of smashers, Joe reported), could be at school in good time with a battery of make-up, to change each person's face into the face it expected to be.

Dan tried to dodge the infection of general excitement but it was no use. He had reached the point now where the play had become more real and important than the world he lived and moved in, and this was confusing and difficult to bear, especially as he didn't want to talk about it to anyone though he suspected most of the others were feeling the same way. He ached for Saturday to come and dreaded the thought of it coming. On Friday night he lay stretched out flat and straight in his bed, thinking of all the last-minute preparations that had gone on in School during the day. Rows of chairs had been set out in the hall and numbered, the scenery was in place, the star had been suspended, the electric switches tested and retested. In the property room, under Miss Hunt's careful direction—she had been ticking off lists and clucking like a hen all week—every costume was checked and laid out, each pair of wings, each robe, each halo teamed and labelled, a last touch of gilt brushed over the crowns, crooks were at the ready, all the garments and cloaks were freshly ironed, an unfamiliar "No Smoking, Please" sign had been hung at the entrance to the hall. A policeman was coming tomorrow afternoon to direct and regulate the traffic. The whole world was coming to school tomorrow, to see the play.

To Dan, still awake in his bed, tomorrow seemed impossible even though it was now so near. The last of this day's trains came in, and the square of light reflected from his mirror shivered on the wallpaper of the opposite wall. The next time the light shivered on the wallpaper would be for the early morning train, and tomorrow would have come at last. But now it was still today and he was still awake.

He must at last have fallen asleep because he dreamed that other unexpected trains came in, train after train after train, so that all the house shook with them, and every train was full of angels, a multitude of the heavenly host stepping out on to the platform and making their way into the town. They thronged the promenade and crowded the pavements, laughing. All the summer amusements had been prepared for them. They set sail on the boating lake and rode on the swing boats with their wings neatly furled. They ate candy floss and ice-cream, they counted the waves and scudded stones and dipped small white feet into the shallow pools that the tide had left as it ran down the sand.

Then from the hills above the town, along every road the shepherds trooped, droves of them, big men in rough homespun cloaks, laughing and talking, each carrying his crook. And the town was filled with shepherds and angels.

Then someone cried, "The Kings! The Kings are coming!" The crowds in the street pressed back to make way for the Kings, and distantly came the steady tramp of camels' feet, the stir of approaching royalty. But just before the camels had come in sight Dan woke up and remembered that this was tomorrow, the day of the play.

"Today's the big day," Mum said at breakfast, and Dan, finding cornflakes spikier than usual, agreed that indeed it was.

"Those crooks were all right, were they?" Dad asked. And Dan, who had told him a dozen times already, told him once again that the shepherds' crooks couldn't have been better. Dad said he was going down to his workshop this morning—twice in the past week the light had been burning in the window as Dan came home from school—but he didn't say anything about coming to the play. Mum was planning to get her shopping over early. That would leave her the whole afternoon to clean up her kitchen—it needed a good clean, she said, and it was going to get it. She liked to leave everything nice before she went out, she said.

Dan imagined her with her hands still red and shiny from the hot water, settling back in her seat, thinking of her spotless kitchen and waiting for the play to begin.

"No need for anyone to be at school before half-past nine," the Headmaster had told them yesterday, but Dan was through the town and halfway up the hill before the town clock stuck nine. Full daylight hadn't come into the sky but already the widened wing of the lighthouse looked pale and faded. The morning was fine and still, spiced with a hint of frost, and shawls of white mist lay against the hill. The donkeys in Big Joe's field were huddled close together, flank to flank, stealing each other's warmth. This morning they didn't disturb themselves to make any check on passersby. Lights in the windows of the scattered houses were going out one by one as daylight strengthened.

Dan wasn't the only person on the road. He thought the figures ahead of him were Sid and Fred, but he made no attempt to catch them up. It was better to be by himself. This time tomorrow, he would be lying in bed smelling Sunday's sausages—Mum always cooked sausages on Sunday—and it would all be over. It would have happened. Meanwhile he stamped his way up the hill, trying by this means to call some confidence into his ankles and into his heart. It wouldn't be Dan Agnew up there on the platform, it would be King Melchior, his crown, his beard, his royal vestments, his precious casket. He wondered how Roger was feeling. Since that evening on the beach nothing else had been said. Roger was avoiding him, Dan thought. He had a deflated air. Certainly Ronnie Simpson seemed happier, more at ease as he went about his page's duties. Roger's face had healed well. At the rehearsal on the day following the fight on the shore Mr Jason Jonson had noticed the cuts and said, "An assassination attempt, I presume, your Majesty?" and Roger had grinned sourly and said, yes, that was what it had been. Dan wondered what lie he and Aunt Florence had found to use to Uncle Bill.

He had almost reached school and could see that the lights in the Hall were burning and that the Headmaster's car was standing outside. There was another car beside it. Dan's heart lurched. It was a police car. Why a police car? Then he remembered, of course a policeman was coming up this afternoon to direct the traffic. Yes, but why should he come this morning? There was nothing to bring a policeman up to school as early as this.

One policeman was stationed at the door into school, and another, talking earnestly to the Headmaster, stood at the inner door leading into the assembly hall. He carried an open notebook. The school caretaker was there too. The Head's face was private and serious.

"No one to go in yet," the policeman at the door told Dan as he pressed forward. Joe and company, storming cheerfully at his back, were also pulled to an abrupt halt.

"No one to come in."

"What's up? Do you know?" Joe inquired. Dan said he didn't, he'd only just come. Something was up, by the look of things.

"No one to go in yet," the policeman at the door said to Roger. Megan had arrived with the pram, and lifted the Kid out, but she too was stopped by the policeman. So were Annette and her bevy of Sob Sisters.

Mr Jason Jonson and Miss Hunt appeared briefly from inside the hall. He looked as if he'd had an encounter with a thunderbolt, and had lost. Miss Hunt's face was pink and her hair stuck up in tails. It was obvious that she had been crying. Mr Jason Jonson passed her his handkerchief.

"What is it? What's been going on?" Roger inquired, and Dan said search him, he'd only just come.

"Keep back there. No one to come in," the policeman at the door warned.

Plainly the Kid didn't care for the look of the policeman and he let out a wail of protest. The Headmaster, glancing up, saw the puzzled crowd halted at the doorway. He said something to the policeman beside him and the policeman nodded and called, "All right, let them come in now. Let them see it for themselves."

They poured across the threshold and stood piled up at the entrance to the Hall, staring. It couldn't be true. Their eyes travelled from the tar-spattered stage to the overturned rows of chairs—there was a liberal sprinkling of tar on them too—and then to the scenery which had been cut into ribbons and hung grotesquely, making a nonsense of itself and all its careful reason and perspective, a jumbled jigsaw of village street and stable, hillside and sky. The star hung crookedly by a single cord. Several of its delicate points had been flattened.

"Look!"

"It's spoiled, it's all spoiled!"

"When? When was it done?"

"First thing this morning the caretaker found it."

"The tar, where did it come from?"

"There was some in the yard, ready for painting the roof of the bicycle shed."

"Our star, our lovely lovely star!"

"Why didn't somebody hear them and make them stop?"

"They were too clever to make any noise, that's why. And it's a long way off the road."

"You'd think somebody would have spotted the light."

"Don't be a loon. Of course they used torches."

"Anyway, they could have done this little job with their eyes half closed."

"Who was it?"

"Who do you think?"

"The Wreckers, you mean?"

"Who else would do a rotten thing like this?"

"I suppose it was their kind of revenge for the time we chased them because they tried to light our bonfire?"

"That's it. The dirty beasts!"

"Our lovely star!"

"Keep back, lads, you don't want to get your feet into that tar," the policeman advised.

They waited, expecting that the Headmaster would make a speech but he just stood there staring at them and at the wreckage. A speech might have helped. It would have let them know what they were supposed to think. It might have eased them a little to hear him expressing his anger in words.

Plainly there was no speech coming. Instead the Head opened the door that led to the property room behind the stage and beckoned to them to come. They walked over warily, dodging the streaks and rivulets of tar.

"You'd better see this too," the Headmaster invited, standing aside so that they could go in.

The confusion in here was worse than the confusion in the Hall and on the stage because it was personal, directed against each one of them. Yesterday all their equipment for the play, their personal furnishing, their second skin, their other self, had lain here in an orderly array, waiting for each actor to claim and inhabit them. This morning everything was scattered in mad disarray, as if a giant had taken a spoon to stir them together. But no giant would have had fingers small enough to do the detailed malicious damage that was done here. The fingers that had done this had enjoyed doing it. Golden crowns were twisted and flattened into cardboard, their jewels lying half in and half out of them. Angels' robes were ripped to tatters, shepherds' cloaks and royal vestments were slit from side to side. Sceptres had been broken in two. Broken arcs from haloes lay in a heap, like pieces of gilded orange skin. Every wing had been torn from top to bottom, and the feather fringe along its edge had been picked off and shredded to bits on the floor. Nothing, not one article except the shepherds' staves had been left unspoiled. The Wreckers had done a thorough job of work.

Miss Hunt had begun to cry again and was looking for a dry place on Mr Jason Jonson's handkerchief.

"There. You can see for yourselves," the Headmaster said, sighing. Mr Jason Jonson didn't speak.

"We'll get them after this little lot, sir, don't you make any mistake about that," one of the policemen said to the Headmaster, but he only nodded absent-mindedly. "Getting them" now wasn't going to be much help.

Surely the Headmaster should have found something to say by this time. He was always able to find words. Speaking was his business. Annette and her friends were already crying quietly. Fat Margie had picked up the pieces of a halo and was trying to fit them together as if it was very important that she should be able to do this. Roger stirred the buckled wreckage of his crown with his toe. The Kid, slumped against Megan's shoulder, was whimpering again but she didn't seem to hear him. It was plain from her tightened face that she wasn't going to cry.

One of the policemen asked the Headmaster where he could use a telephone, and the Headmaster invited him to come with him to his study. "I'll be back in a moment or two," he told the cast. Miss Hunt and Mr Jason Jonson followed him from the Hall.

It was a long time before anybody spoke. There should have been a great deal to say but little of it seemed now to be worth saying. Faced with this devastation it was almost too much trouble to be angry. Anger wouldn't help. Nothing would help. It had happened, that was all. Early this morning, while they had been still in bed perhaps, or had just woken and

148

remembered what day it was, this was happening up here in the Hall. And it was all finished now.

People at last began to talk, not all together, but in jerky sequences as if they were throwing a ball about. Roger started it. "That's that then," he said, giving his crown a final kick. "They certainly made a good job of it."

"The Oldies will have to be told. They were having their tea early so that they could come. Matron said they could have it early."

"Everyone will have to be told."

"Our lovely wings!"

"The kids in the First Form have been ticking off the days."

"My Dad had got the afternoon off, special."

"The star, did you see what they'd done to the star?"

"Miss Hunt had been crying."

"That lot won't half be pleased with themselves."

"They'll be laughing their heads off."

"They must have cut the cloaks with scissors. They must have brought scissors to do it, specially."

"She'd ironed them all yesterday."

"My kid sister was coming."

"They must have brought the scissors with them."

The Headmaster, with Miss Hunt and Mr Jason Jonson, came back into the Hall. He held up his hand for silence though there wasn't any need, no one was talking now. The Headmaster had found words at last.

"You will all have been as shocked and distressed by what has occurred as we are," he said, "and you will realize what it means. Even if it had been possible to

clean up the stage and the seating in the Hall in time,
you have seen that the scenery and costumes and other
essential properties have been damaged beyond repair.
In these circumstances there is nothing we can do
except to cancel the performance of the play."

No one moved. No one spoke. Mr Jason Jonson
stared at the floor, Miss Hunt allowed tears to drip un-
mopped on to her crocheted jersey. If they had heard
the Headmaster saying this a few weeks ago they would
have been grateful from the bottom of their hearts. But
they weren't grateful now.

Dan heard his own voice before he realized that he
intended to speak.

"Please, sir!"

"Yes, Dan, what is it?"

"I think we should still do the play, sir."

The Headmaster's eyebrows zipped up into his hair
and stayed there. "Still do the play? Don't be a fool,
boy, how can you? You've seen what has happened."

"Please, sir!"

This time it was Roger. Of course it would be Roger,
Roger out to make a fool of Dan, those two never
missed an opportunity of getting at each other. The
rest of the company waited with interest to hear what
kind of mincemeat Roger had in mind this time. It
would be good.

"Well, Roger?"

"Please, sir, I think Dan's right."

"You—what?"

Roger swallowed hard. "We could still do the play,
sir, without the properties or the scenery."

"Without——?"

To have Roger ganging up on the same side as Dan was as surprising as the cause they were promoting.

Roger went on, "Properties and scenery don't really matter. It's the play and the people who are important. Mr Jason Jonson told us that, sir."

The Headmaster raised his eyes to the ceiling as if asking heaven for strength and reason and then focused them on Mr Jason Jonson who had lifted his gaze from the floor and was staring delightedly at Roger.

"Go on," Roger demanded, "tell him what you told us."

"Tell him," they insisted.

"The play is the actors, Headmaster," Mr Jason Jonson said. It was what they had been waiting for. "That's right, we're the play," they agreed, grinning.

No one could have explained why this had happened or why it was now enormously important that the play should be performed. It wasn't just to spite the Wreckers or to please Mr Jason Jonson and Miss Hunt, or because the Oldies were looking forward to it so much, or because the youngest classes had been ticking off the days. It was important because this was Christmas and Christmas was what the play was about.

The Headmaster took his glasses off and made a lengthy business of polishing them. "You've all seen the state of the stage and the seating, you know it wouldn't be possible to clean them up in time."

Roger said, "We don't have to do it in the Hall, sir."

"You—what?"

Dan told him, "Roger said we don't have to do it in the Hall."

"Then perhaps you'll tell me where you propose the performance should be given." The Headmaster was recovering his form now. He smiled. He knew he held all the top cards.

Neither Dan nor Roger had an answer. Their faces reddened. Roger mumbled something inaudible and seemed to sag. "You will agree that a hall is necessary?" the Headmaster said.

Joe spoke up from the back. "Please, sir!"

The Headmaster's smile was peeled off his face. He was getting tired of this. Let the kids clear off home and the police could get on with their job, the sooner they got at it the better.

"Well, Joe, what is it?"

"Please, sir, there's my Dad's big barn. We could do the play there."

"Your Dad's big barn? Whatever are you talking about?"

"The barn in the donkeys' field, sir. There's plenty of room there and it's dry and out of the cold. My Dad has sold all the hay except what he keeps for the donkeys during the winter. We could use those bales for seats and for marking out the stage. It'd be just right, you'll see."

The Headmaster must have been aware of the sudden breeze of hope that stirred through the Hall and blew in all their faces. His tone grew more tough, more official. "Have some sense, boy. You know as well as I do it gets dark long before evening."

Joe's expression was that of an inspired mule. "We could put the play forward till two o'clock. If we started at two it would give us plenty of light."

"And what do you propose to do about the dress rehearsal?"

"No need for it, sir. And with the costumes and props gone we couldn't have a dress rehearsal anyway."

Excitement mounted as Joe and the Headmaster exchanged thrust for thrust. One of them was talking utter and complete nonsense, the question was—which of them was it?

"And what do you think your father would have to say?" the Headmaster challenged. "How would he like the whole of the school and most of the town piling into his barn?"

This was surely a trump card. Big Joe was never short of words or afraid to use them. Most of the children had been chased off his property at one time or another, and had been lucky to reach the hedge before any of his threats could be carried out.

"Well?" smiled the Headmaster.

Every eye was turned on Joe. "I'll fix it with my Dad," he declared. It wasn't a promise or a boast, certainly not a threat, it was simply a statement of fact. Assuredly Joe would fix it with Big Joe.

And as soon as Joe had finished speaking everybody in the Hall—including the Headmaster and Mr Jason Jonson, whose eyes now blazed with joy—knew that the School Play would be performed in Big Joe's barn at two o'clock in the afternoon.

❊ *Chapter Ten*

"Two o'clock!" Dan's Mum declared, "I never heard of such a thing!" She was swilling the dinner dishes through the hot soapy water like fury. A jungle of saucepans and bowls, rolling pin, chopping board—she baked every Saturday morning after she'd done the shopping—waited at her elbow. Cutlery lay jumbled in a greasy heap until she was ready to deal with it. "Two o'clock! It's crazy! Nobody'll ever make it by two o'clock, you wouldn't expect them. And up in Big Joe's barn at this time of year! They'll catch their deaths!"

The last of the dinner plates had been washed. Mum changed the water in the basin and threw in the cutlery noisily to show her contempt for the alteration in plans.

"That's when it's to be anyway," Dan said dispiritedly. He ought to have expected it would be like this, but he had been carried along by the urgent need to perform this play which had infected them all.

Dad was tying his shoes, his best shoes, making sure the laces lay straight and even, the way he used to tie them for Church on Sundays, or in the evenings long ago when he and Mum went out visiting. Did this mean——? "It would need to be two o'clock because of the light," Dad said, as if Mum would have to have it explained to her.

"If you'd told me sooner," Mum moaned, "I might have made plans. But coming home as late as this and springing it on me——"

"I couldn't get home to tell you any sooner, Mum. We've been at it all morning in the barn, setting up the bales of hay and putting things right."

The boys had made a good job of the barn. They had built low walls of hay bales along the unwalled side, leaving only sufficient space for the audience to enter. They had set more bales in a semicircle around the area where the choir and the recorder players would be stationed and where the action would take place. Another couple of rows of bales had been added to provide seats for senior spectators, everyone else would have to sit on the ground. The donkeys, puzzled and nervous with all this activity, had withdrawn in a huddle to the field's farther corner.

Meanwhile the girls had scattered to visit any household in the town which might not otherwise have heard the news, and Mrs Hutchin had put up a notice in the window of the Post Office—"School Play—Two o'clock—Up in Big Joe's barn." The news had been passed on by the postman, by bus conductors, in shops and in the barber's, and Mr Hibbert had toured the outlying villages on his motor-bike, taking the school loudhailer with him. The Oldies had persuaded Matron to provide lunch half an hour early instead of changing the time of tea. Big Joe's barn? Yes, they would come, of course they would. Rugs and mufflers, lined boots, hoods and excitement would defeat the weather. They would certainly be there. The members of the school who were to have attended the dress rehearsal would be able to crowd in and find places on the wide floor of the barn, in front of the seated audience. There would be room for everybody.

"You won't need to keep a place for me, that's one sure thing," Mum said, reaching for the washing-up liquid again. "By the time I've got this lot sorted up and the kitchen cleaned the way I clean it it will be past four, if I know anything about it."

A train went by, the kitchen was filled with the noise of it and the washing-up water rocked in the basin. That would be the one thirty-seven. Dan's heart sank lower than ever. Mum seemed to relish the effort that all this disorder offered her, as if by putting her kitchen back to its neat immaculate self she proved something, something that was important to her.

"How could I walk out on all this?" she challenged him.

How could she? "I'll have to go on then," Dan said. He knew it was hopeless.

Surprisingly Dad spoke. "We may as well come with you, Dan. Fetch your hat and coat, Doris."

Mum gaped across her confusion of implements and the kitchen that showed up a day's traffic. "I told you. I can't come!"

"You're coming." Dad wasn't asking, he was telling her.

"And leave things in this state? What are you talking about, some women might, but not me. I'd never enjoy a moment of it, you know I wouldn't. And I can read all about it in the paper afterwards, and Dan and you can tell me."

"Hurry now and fetch your things. We've barely got twenty minutes."

Dan's mother lifted her hands out of the hot water and they dripped and steamed while she stared at her husband. It seemed as if she couldn't believe that he was speaking to her like this. Dan could hardly believe it either. His heart ached for Mum to come. Remember what I told you about Baboushka. Of course you must come! Think of Baboushka. Don't let your chance slip away as hers had done.

Still looking at Dad Mum walked to the towel that hung behind the door and dried her hands on it slowly. Then she smiled at him and went off into the bedroom.

"You'd best get on ahead," Dad said to Dan. "I'll see to it that your Mum and I are up in good time."

And Dan, with his heart full of joy and miracles cartwheeling on all sides of him, went on up to school by himself.

Before two o'clock everyone had arrived in Big Joe's barn and the play was ready to begin. They had come in cars, on foot, on bicycles, a couple of taxis, a minibus. The whole of the neighbourhood was there.

Mr Jason Jonson, with humble pride, spoke the prologue and asked the audience to join in singing with the choir the first of the carols.

> *"O come, all ye faithful,*
> *Joyful and triumphant,*
> *Come ye, o come ye, to Bethlehem."*

Bethlehem was in the barn in Big Joe's field. Players and audience stood up to sing and then the play began.

The first scene was the bringing of the news to Mary by the Angel Gabriel. No one needed to be told that Pete was the Angel Gabriel. He had all the authority and dignity of his office. Of course he was the Angel Gabriel, who else could he have been?

> *"In Bethlehem's city, in Jewry it was,*
> *That Joseph and Mary together did pass,*
> *All for to be taxed when thither they came,*
> *For Caesar Augustus commanded the same.*
> *But when they had come to the city so fair*
> *A number of people so mighty was there*
> *That Joseph and Mary, whose substance was small*
> *Could find in the inn there no lodging at all."*

Here were the thronged streets of Bethlehem. Here were the tired travellers turned away from the inn, looking for refuge in a stable.

> *"Their lodging so simple they took it no scorn,*
> *And against the next morning our Saviour was born!"*

Here was the stable. Now the child had been laid in the manger, Mary and Joseph rested beside him.

Now it was the turn of the recorders with the Pastoral Symphony. Every note was true. Moonlight shone and shivered on the grass of the hillsides around Bethlehem.

And there were the shepherds, tending their sheep, with the night sky darkening above them.

> "Hark the herald angels sing
> Glory to the newborn King!"

Suddenly one angel and then all the company of angels had come with their joyful news. The spectators knew that their unseen wings and haloes were a hundred times more beautiful than anything plastic or gilt paint could ever have produced. Their glory filled Big Joe's barn. The shepherds bent their heads and shielded their eyes from the light.

> "Say, ye holy shepherds say
> What your joyful news today?
> Wherefore have you left your sheep
> On the lonely mountain steep?"

The shepherds had come with great joy and had found Mary and Joseph, and the young child lying in a manger.

> "We three Kings of Orient are,
> Bearing gifts we traverse afar,
> Field and fountain, moor and mountain,
> Following yonder star."

Caspar, Baltazar and Melchior had alighted from their camels and advanced with their pages in attendance to offer gifts to the child. Plainly the gifts they had brought were kings' gifts, fit for a king. They knelt, Caspar the magnificent, Baltazar the mysterious, Melchior, old, wise and frail, undoubted kings, paying tribute.

The play was nearly over now, but the players knew that they had been building a bridge, a bridge between themselves and the little kids squatting wide-eyed in the front row, between themselves and the rest of the school crowded in behind, between themselves and the Mums and Dads who were joining in the choruses of the carols, between themselves and the Oldies, huddled in hoods and scarves, with rugs slung across their shoulders, watching with solemn joy.

And the name of the bridge was Christmas. Christmas had come because the children were there and children will always bring Christmas.

"Ding dong merrily on high,
In heaven the bells are ringing."

And ding dong merrily in Big Joe's barn from angels, shepherds, kings, pages, the recorders going full blast, the music master with the glockenspiel beating out the bells.

Outside the barn the winter afternoon had begun to fade. The donkeys had come to the entrance and stood thrusting inquisitive noses across the bales of hay, nudging each other and jostling. The child in the manger whimpered, and Megan, who had become Mary, leaned forward to pull the shawl a little more closely around him.